Fetterman moved toward Gerber, then froze

There was a crackling sound, like someone walking through the jungle. The master sergeant knew that Gerber wouldn't be making any noise, if he happened to be moving. Fetterman glanced to the right, and when their eyes met, he pointed at the sound and Gerber nodded. Slowly the captain pulled his knife, holding it up for Fetterman to see.

Fetterman followed suit, then knelt, waiting. Through a gap in the vegetation, he caught a glimpse of a khaki uniform and an AK-47.

Both he and Gerber were hidden, and the soldier coming at them had no reason to suspect they were there. Then the enemy stopped. There was no sound or movement. Fetterman could see a single shoulder glistening in the sun, as if the soldier had taken off the shirt.

A moment later the figure bent forward, and Fetterman realized it was a woman. She was now completely naked. He couldn't believe the timing. Another few minutes and he would have been gone. Now the woman stood between him and the captain.

Suddenly she started straight toward him. There wasn't a thing Fetterman could do about it.

He raised the knife slowly....

VIETNAM: GROUND ZERO T.M.

DRAGON'S JAW

ERIC HELM

A GOLD EAGLE BOOK FROM
WORLDWIDE ®

TORONTO · NEW YORK · LONDON · PARIS
AMSTERDAM · STOCKHOLM · HAMBURG
ATHENS · MILAN · TOKYO · SYDNEY

First edition February 1989

ISBN 0-373-62716-5

VIETNAM: GROUND ZERO™

DRAGON'S JAW

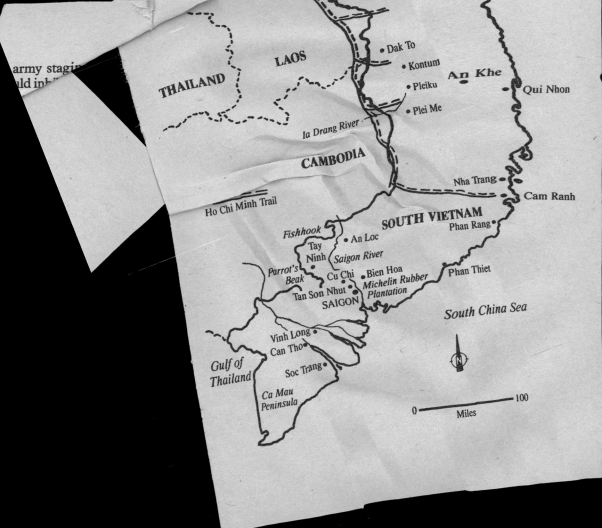

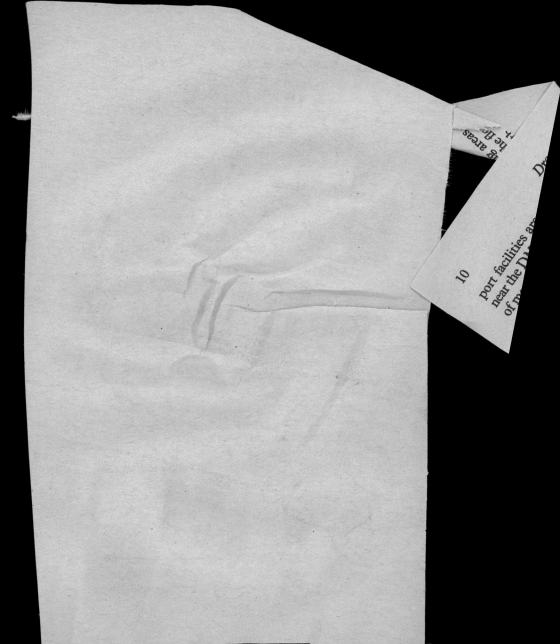

10

port facilities are
near the D
of m

PROLOGUE

OVER NORTH VIETNAM

Below him, through a broken mass of clouds, were the deep greens of North Vietnam. At twenty-five thousand feet, with an intermittent undercast that stretched toward the horizon like a dirty, lumpy blanket, Air Force Captain Lawrence Kincaid felt safe for the moment. The enemy would know that he was coming—they could hear his engines and they could see his plane through the broken clouds—but they wouldn't be shooting at him. Yet.

Kincaid was belted into the cockpit of his fighter, held in place by the equipment he wore and all the instruments and controls of the aircraft. He was dressed in a one-piece Nomex flying suit that made him hot and miserable because it didn't allow his skin to breathe. He also wore an anti-G suit, flight helmet and gloves. The tensions of flying and not being able to move anything except his hands and feet made the chore that much worse. His thighs, hips and shoulders ached. The sweatband around his head had been soaked almost from the moment he'd taken off from Da Nang.

He, along with a flight of three other fighters, continued north along the coast toward the Thanh Hoa railroad and highway bridge. It was one of the major arteries to the South and it connected the manufacturing centers around Hanoi, the port facilities around Haiphong and the army staging areas near the DMZ. If it was knocked out, it would inhibit the flow of men, arms, ammunition and equipment to the South.

That was the theory in Saigon and confirmed by the intelligence analysis handed out by the Pentagon. It also explained why Kincaid and his wingmen were flying north to bomb it out of existence.

They stayed above the clouds, watching for MiGs, which had become fewer as the airwar expanded. Kincaid swiveled his head repeatedly, watching the sky and then the ground. So far everything was clear, and Kincaid took the last few moments to relax slightly.

When they were only minutes from the bridge site, Kincaid began a slow descent through the clouds. The sunlight was cut down and then, as they penetrated a mist that seemed to be rolling in from the coast, it faded away. It was as if they had traveled from one world into another, from bright sunlight into the rainy swamps of Venus.

Radio traffic was kept to a minimum. Each of the men in the flight of four knew what his job was. Each could see the other, with the exception of the leader, who couldn't see everyone. But then each of them had done it all before, flying into the clouds of flak and fountains of tracers near the Thanh Hoa bridge. And now, with the deployment of the SA-2 Guideline, there were SAM missiles to worry about.

"Got triple A to the right," said one of the men.

Kincaid glanced in that direction and saw a string of tracers burning brightly in the mist. They were aimed poorly, well away from the flight.

"More on the left," said another.

And then, over the radio, he heard the buzz of a field phone. That meant he was being tracked by radar, probably 37 or 57 mm.

"Breaking right."

As he spoke, he turned abruptly, dived and then leveled off. It was enough to break the radar lock. Outside, the mist had thickened into a rain shower that obscured the ground in curtains of gray and black.

Ahead of them was the Thanh Hoa bridge. Thinly veiled, it stood out suddenly as the rain let up and the sun popped through, almost as if to spotlight the target for them. Thanh Hoa stretched across the Song Ma River almost from north to south. There were railroad tracks on one side and a highway on the other. Surrounding it, now that the Americans were interested in it, were the antiaircraft defenses. First were the ZSU-23s, both the twin-barreled, optically sighted version and the four-barreled, radar-controlled weapon. Along with them were the 37 and 57 mm weapons that were effective to nearly twenty thousand feet. Finally there were the SAM missiles. They weren't effective below two thousand feet, but were good up to nearly a hundred thousand. The combined missiles gave the enemy an effective envelope of coverage from the ground to a level far above the service ceiling of the fighter Kincaid flew.

Again the field phone rang, but there was nothing Kincaid could do about it now. Lines of tracers rose up at him, moving first with exaggerated slow motion and then whipping by. Kincaid ignored them. Instead, he kept his eyes on the bridge just visible in front of him.

Now the sky became thicker with more tracers, some of them green but many of them red. Those that were far off looked small, almost festive, but those coming up at him seemed to loom larger than basketballs—huge glowing balls of death that would shred his airplane.

The radio was alive with chatter as the men called out the enemy gunners. No longer did Kincaid have the luxury of flying straight at the target. He dodged and weaved through the sky, trying to make it impossible for the enemy to hit him. He trusted the flight to stay with him. Clouds of flak, small puffs of black smoke, began to appear around him. The enemy was serious.

"Got guns to the right."

"Light guns on the left."

"I have a SAM indication."

"Keep it together. Target in sight."

Kincaid then began a rapid climb, gaining back the altitude he'd lost trying to avoid the enemy's antiaircraft. He lined up on the bridge, using the center of it as his aiming point. Once that was established, he rolled over and released the bombs. As soon as they were away, he climbed again, rolling to the right and away from the target.

The flak was suddenly thicker, punching holes in the clouds and rain. Tracers from machine guns and small arms came up out of the semidarkness that draped some of the landscape. Kincaid rolled right and then left, trying to avoid it all.

Less than a minute later the last pilot in the flight said, "We're all clear."

"Go to afterburners," said Kincaid.

"You're joined."

"Roger. How'd it look back there?"

"I don't think we got it."

Kincaid wanted to punch something. He wanted to close his eyes and clench his fists, but couldn't. He had to keep flying the airplane, knowing that he would have to go back and try again, just as the enemy knew he would be back.

"Roger," said Kincaid. "Beginning a slow climb."

Moments later they were crossing the coast of North Vietnam and were suddenly out over the South China Sea.

"Out of burners."

"We going to have to go back, Skipper?"

Kincaid didn't like the question because the enemy might be listening. There was no reason to give them any answers that they didn't already have. "We do any damage?"

"That's a negative. Cratered the approaches and may have dropped a single span. Railroad bridge is intact."

Kincaid wanted to swear. He wanted to scream. Instead he said, "Roger. Understood."

Without saying any more, he turned south and continued the climb. As he reached altitude, in the clear blue sky, leaving the rain and mist behind him, Kincaid realized how tense he had been. He relaxed and felt the tension drain out of him.

What he didn't say to the men of his flight was that they would have to go back. The bridge had to be destroyed, and it would stay on the target lists until they removed it by dropping it into the Song Ma.

To himself he muttered, "I hope someone figures out something before we have to go back." There was a job he didn't want to do. The enemy had too many guns defending the bridge. Something else would have to be figured out.

1

THE CARASEL HOTEL
SAIGON

For the past three days Army Special Forces Captain MacKenzie K. Gerber had been lounging around the hotel in Saigon, his idleness the result of a hairy mission and the lack of coordination by the brass at both MACV Headquarters and MACV-SOG. Neither group had been prepared for Gerber, along with Master Sergeant Anthony B. Fetterman, to drop in on them, so no one had an assignment in mind for them. Gerber, wise to the ways of the American military command in Vietnam, had thanked them and then gotten out before someone thought of something.

Now, having hidden out for three days in the Carasel Hotel, eating the best food and relaxing in the facilities available, he was beginning to feel guilty. Not enough to call in to find out if anyone had thought of something for him to do, but enough to worry about it periodically.

Fetterman, on the other hand, having been broken of the habit of using the quarters supplied at Tan Son Nhut, wasn't feeling guilty. The master sergeant, a diminutive balding man, was enjoying the luxury of the hotel. He ordered huge breakfasts and then ate them slowly, savoring each course. He drank gallons of fresh fruit juice, something that wasn't available to the men in the field, even when the field was the huge American base at Cu Chi.

Gerber had accompanied Fetterman down to breakfast. He sat opposite him now, digging into a meal of steak, eggs, hash browns and orange juice. Gerber was a tall, thin man with a deep tropical tan. He was just over thirty and had combat experience in both Korea and Vietnam. Like Fetterman, who had been a kid crossing Omaha Beach in the Second World War, Gerber had been a kid fighting in Korea. Once that was over, he had attended college, studying botany because it had seemed like the thing to do at the time. But he had also enrolled in ROTC, graduating with a commission in the Army Reserve.

Now, dressed in new jungle fatigues that bore no insignia, Gerber ate quietly, glancing at the *Stars and Stripes* that lay folded on the table. "Says here," he told Fetterman, "that the South Vietnamese have acquired the capacity to maintain their own security and that they're going to take over more and more of the fighting."

Fetterman buttered a piece of toast and nodded. "It say *when* they're going to take over more and more of the fighting?"

"Nope," said Gerber. "Just that they have the capacity to do so, not that they will."

"Well," said Fetterman, rocking back in his chair and pushing his plate aside, "I don't think it's something we need to worry about now."

Gerber closed his paper and dropped it onto the floor, out of the way. As he continued to eat his breakfast, he said, "You see how staying out of sight keeps us from ending up with lousy assignments? They can't find you and they can't assign you."

Just as he finished speaking, Justin Tyme appeared in the doorway. Tyme was a young sandy-haired kid who had a love of weapons and who had served as Gerber's light-weapons specialist during his first tour. He stood there for a moment, searching the room.

"I don't like the looks of this," said Gerber.

Fetterman turned and looked at Tyme. "Maybe he's just hungry."

"I don't think so. He's looking for us. There, he's seen us and is coming this way."

Tyme stopped at the table. "Morning, Captain, Master Sergeant."

"Justin, have a seat."

"Well, sir, I was sent over here to find you."

Gerber plucked the napkin from his lap and wiped his lips. He dropped it onto the table and looked up at the sergeant. "How'd they know we were here?"

Tyme grinned. "I don't think they did. They sent a bunch of us out with instructions to locate you and inform you that you're required at a briefing at MACV-SOG at 1300 hours today."

Gerber looked at his watch. "You want some breakfast, Justin?"

"Breakfast would be nice."

"You have any clue why they want to see us?" asked Fetterman.

"No, Tony, I don't. Just said that an important briefing was going to be held at 1300 and that both of you were supposed to be there."

Gerber picked up his juice and drained the glass. He set it down carefully, then looked at the table—a real tablecloth, linen napkins, silverware that gleamed and glass made of crystal. It was much nicer than anything he'd see in the field, where a soldier got steel trays and cutlery made of aluminum. He pushed his plate away. "I'm suddenly not very hungry."

"You have a clue, Captain?" asked Fetterman.

"No. It's just like always. Some brass hat has a wild hair and we're the only people who can handle it."

Fetterman laughed. "Maybe it's an awards ceremony and they're going to give us medals."

"When was the last time anyone in the military ever did anything like that for you?"

"Good point," said Fetterman.

"We'll just have to wait until one o'clock and see what they want."

KINCAID SAT in the tiny office that contained only a gray metal desk, a metal folding chair and a settee that had been repaired with black tape. The walls were plywood that had been scorched by a blowtorch and then varnished. Halfway to the corrugated tin roof the walls ended, giving way to screening. A ceiling fan spun rapidly, creating a breeze that didn't really cool. The humid tropical air seemed to hold the moisture like a wet towel that blanketed everything.

Sitting in front of Kincaid was a man wearing a one-piece flying suit, the leaves of a colonel encased in plastic sewn to the shoulders. Lieutenant Colonel Bruce Johnson was a tall, spare man with short-cropped graying hair. He looked boyish, despite the wrinkles around his blue eyes, and though he had been in-country for nearly six months, his face was sunburned as if he had just arrived.

After waiting a moment, Kincaid said, "I don't like being summoned here like this. I've got a job to do in Da Nang, sir."

Johnson picked a pack of cigarettes off the desk in front of him and shook one out. He tapped it against the desk and put it between his lips. With his left hand, which was still bandaged from the flash fire in the cockpit two weeks earlier, he patted his pockets until he located his matches. When he got the cigarette lighted, he puffed a lungful of smoke at the ceiling fan and then demanded, "Who asked for your opinion?"

"Sir?"

Although the cigarette didn't need it, Johnson flicked the ash to the floor and repeated impatiently, "Who asked your opinion? You were ordered here for a debriefing, not to offer your opinion."

Kincaid was surprised by that. He blinked rapidly and tried to think of what to say. The last thing he wanted was to get into a pissing contest with a superior officer, but he didn't like the man's attitude. Finally, because he could think of nothing that wouldn't get him into trouble, he said, "Yes, sir."

Johnson opened a manila folder that was sitting on his desk. "All right. Now, I see from the latest bomb damage assessment that we had almost no luck with the bridge at Thanh Hoa."

"No, sir." Kincaid wanted to offer a few reasons why they had failed to destroy it, but didn't want to give Johnson another reason for coming down on him.

"Why is that?"

"Simple. It's damned hard to hit something with any degree of accuracy when it's only fifty or seventy feet wide. Add in the winds, which we can only guess at, and the fact that the entire North Vietnamese army is trying to shoot holes in your airplane, and the task becomes that much more difficult."

Johnson flipped the folder shut and stared into Kincaid's face. "You telling me you can't do the job?"

"No, sir. I'm telling you the problems of doing the job right. The enemy knows we want that bridge, and they're doing everything they can to keep us from getting it."

"So what's the problem?"

Kincaid felt himself grow cold with sudden anger. He wanted to hit Johnson in the face. "The problem is that we don't dedicate the force necessary to do the job. We're going about it in the same half-assed way we're running all aspects of the war."

"Uh-huh," said Johnson, nodding.

"Sir, if I may be frank, what we need is a suppression flight in there first. Maybe two. One to hit the triple A and one to keep the SAMs busy. While that was going on, we could hit the bridge, taking the time we need to set it up. Given that, we shouldn't have a problem."

Johnson finished his cigarette and crushed it out on the side of his desk. He dropped the butt onto the floor. "Then you're blaming your failure on a number of factors, none of which you control."

"Sir?"

"You've already said you don't have sufficient force to do the job, which translates as a lack of command emphasis.

You've suggested the weather hasn't been as predicted, blaming the forecasters here in the South, and you've blamed the heavy antiaircraft artillery that surrounds the site."

Kincaid sat up for a moment and finally nodded. "Yes, sir, that about sums it up."

"Then it's not your fault."

"No, sir. I could do the job if I had the men and equipment to do it, and I didn't have to worry about a half-dozen pages of restricted targets."

"All right, Captain, I think I have a clear picture of the whole situation. I'll want you at a briefing this afternoon at 1300. At that time I'll want you to relate everything you've told me. Hold nothing back. It'll allow us to come up with a plan that'll ensure the destruction of the bridge."

"Yes, sir."

"Until that time I don't want you talking with anyone about what was said in here. Understood?"

"Yes, sir."

TWELVE THOUSAND MILES AWAY, the interior of the conference room was unnaturally cold. Even though the outdoor temperature in San Francisco wasn't that high, the air conditioner was running in an attempt to filter the growing cloud of cigarette smoke from the room. Sitting around the small conference table, in low-backed chairs covered with cigarette burns, were seven people—five men and two women. On the walls of the room were large color photographs of the important stories the reporters had covered in the past couple of years, including the war in Vietnam, violent crime in the United States and one spectacular fire in San Francisco.

Carla Phillips and Richard Travis sat on one side of the table, facing the other five people. In front of them was a single sheet of paper on which they had scribbled their notes just prior to the meeting.

Phillips was a short, slender woman with short dark hair. She had blue eyes, an angular face and a pointed nose and was dressed in jeans and an old University of California at Berkeley sweatshirt.

Travis was a tall, stout man who had grown a beard in the past six months to prove he was a radical. There were flecks of gray in it. His hair was long and shaggy. He wore a blue work shirt that was frayed at the collar and jeans that were bleached nearly white. Since he was never seen on camera, it didn't make any difference how he looked.

Those opposite Phillips and Travis were all dressed in suits and ties, or in the case of Sarah Romig, a high-necked dress. Their hair was groomed and none of the men had any facial hair.

The assignment editor, Ralph Chapman, tapped on the legal pad that sat in front of him. He scanned his notes as he puffed on a cigarette. "Let me see if I have this straight. The invitation was routed through the Soviet Trade Delegation?"

"Yes. A formal document that Mr. Lucero has in his office now," Phillips said. She snatched her cigarette from the overflowing ashtray, puffed once and put it down again. With the back of her hand, she brushed at the hair hanging over her forehead.

"I'm inclined to say no," said Chapman.

"Why in hell would you want to do that?" demanded Travis. "This is the perfect opportunity for us, one that'll allow us to beat the pants off the competition."

"They don't have this?" asked Chapman.

"As far as I know," said Travis, "we're alone, but if we don't get back to them, they'll extend the invitation to someone else and we'll be out in the cold."

"Have either of you worked out an itinerary or a budget for this?"

"Budget would be for the airfare and the cost of the crew to go with us. On the other hand, we'll have an exclusive that we can cut into a five- or ten-part series to air in May for the sweeps, and then we'll be able to recut for a half-hour or hour documentary for July. We'll get a lot of mileage out of this," said Travis.

Chapman scratched the back of his head and turned to Romig. "What do you think, Sarah?"

She leaned back in her chair and clasped her hands behind her head. "Well, I don't like the hole this is going to create in our news budget, but then such an opportunity doesn't come along very often." She looked pointedly at Phillips. "Anything been said about your safety during this trip?"

"I think that's going to be the least of our troubles," said Phillips. "The last thing these people are going to want is for one of us to get hurt or killed while there."

"Have you checked into getting the necessary visas and entrance papers?"

Travis took over. "Not yet, but since the invitation was extended at the request of their government, I can't see that as being a major problem."

Romig looked back to Chapman and shrugged. "I still don't know."

Chapman glanced at his notepad. "Does anyone else have any other questions?"

The man at the far end, an older man with short hair, a dark blue suit and white shirt, said, "I've got just one. Did anyone here, meaning any of our people, check with the State Department to get their reaction to this invitation?"

Travis scratched his head and kept his eyes on the ashtray in front of him. "We haven't done that yet because we haven't made a decision here."

"Wouldn't you suspect that their reaction is going to be less than enthusiastic?"

"Come on, Paul," said Chapman. "We can't let the State Department, or any other branch of the government, decide what we're going to put on our newscasts. We have a responsibility to the people to let them know what's happening."

"There's a point when that comes into direct conflict with what's good for the country. Sometimes you can't have it both ways."

"This isn't the time nor the place for a debate on the responsibilities of the press," said Chapman.

"Excuse me, I thought you'd brought up that issue."

"The issue before this meeting is whether or not to accept the invitation. Now, if there are no other questions."

"Just one. What's the reaction of the Pentagon?"

"Oh, for Christ's sake, Paul, will you get off that high horse? We're not going to run to the Pentagon, or the State Department for that matter, to get permission like some little kid who wants to cross the street to go to the park. We're going to make our decision and then inform the various authorities to secure the paperwork. Now, is there anything else?" Chapman's voice had taken on a hard edge.

"What will be the makeup of the team we send?" Romig asked.

"I thought that was obvious from the start," Phillips said. "I'll be going as the field correspondent, Dick here as the producer and we'll take a camera and sound crew from the pool."

"No," said Paul. "I don't like this at all."

"Why not?" snapped Phillips. "Because I happen to be female?"

Paul began to shake his head and then stopped. "I'm afraid that is it."

"Well, you can forget about that, Schaffer," she shot back. "Won't hold water. Women have been involved in the worst of the stories for a long time now, and I'll be safer than the women assigned to the bureaus in South Vietnam."

Chapman interrupted. "I think we can end the debate right now. If we decide to send in people, Phillips will be the correspondent. There's no reason to take her out of the picture. If there's nothing else . . ."

Travis looked as if he was going to speak but then didn't. He plucked a cigarette from the pack lying on the table in front of him and lighted it.

"All right," said Chapman. "Unless someone objects, I'm going to approve this plan and take it to the station manager. He'll have to give final approval."

"I don't like us having to get permission from him for a news story," Travis said.

Chapman grinned. "We're not getting permission to do the story. We're getting permission to spend the money to get the story."

"Same thing."

"Not really. If we show that the story's important, he'll approve the budget. Now, any objections?"

"Yes," said Schaffer. "I don't like this one bit. It smacks of giving aid and comfort to the enemy."

"Oh, Christ, Schaffer," said Chapman. "We're just trying to do a story here and give the people a complete picture of the war in Vietnam. We're not trying to overthrow the government of the United States. Now, if no one else objects, then the story is approved."

He waited and then slapped the table. "All right, that's it. Carla, put on your walking shoes. You're on your way."

Phillips snatched her cigarette from the ashtray, took a long drag on it, then crushed it out. As she exhaled the smoke, she stood and said, "You won't be disappointed."

"I know. How can we miss? The first pictures of the destruction of Hanoi by the Americans. People are going to sit up and take notice."

Phillips smiled broadly and repeated, "How can we miss?"

2

MACV-SOG
TAN SON NHUT AIR BASE
SAIGON

Gerber stood outside the single-story building with the corrugated tin roof and looked toward the airfield where two Phantoms were roaring down the runway. The rumbling of their engines overpowered all other sound, and the twin trails of black smoke from their engines drifted on a light crosswind. Gerber could smell the partially burnt kerosene as it mingled with the odors of South Vietnam.

Since the Americans had arrived in force after the Gulf of Tonkin resolution had been passed, they had been adding to the stench in the atmosphere of South Vietnam. With a water table that was so high that much of the country was under water, there was nothing to do except burn the raw sewage of a hundred thousand outhouses. Daily.

Vietnamese workers pulled the drums from under the outhouses, mixed in kerosene and set them on fire. Black smoke from them hung in the air and the pungent odor from them invaded everywhere. It was as prevalent as the heat and humidity and the fumes of the jet engines.

When the Phantoms disappeared and all that remained were the twin trails of black smoke, the rest of the noise of Tan Son

Nhut assaulted Gerber—the whump of helicopter rotor blades and the roar of transport engines. In the distance was the boom of artillery as one of the many fire support bases tried to eliminate the unseen enemy hiding in the rice paddies and fingers of jungle around Saigon.

Gerber turned and looked at the small building, which consisted of sandbags, plywood and screen. The sandbags were the new rubberized kind that had a glowing green all their own. The plywood was unpainted and the screen was beginning to rust in the humid environment of South Vietnam.

"Going to be a hot one," said Fetterman, rubbing his face with a handkerchief that was already soaked with sweat.

Gerber nodded and wiped his face. There were stains under his arms and down his back. "Be a day to move slow in the boondocks. Heat seems worse."

A jeep pulled up then and Jerry Maxwell, the local CIA man, got out. Maxwell was a tall, skinny man who looked uncomfortable in the tropics. He had been in Saigon for nearly two years but still hadn't gotten used to the heat. As usual, he wore his standard uniform of white suit, white shirt and loosened thin black tie. His black hair was plastered to his head, making it seem as if he had just stepped out of the shower. "Gentlemen," he said.

"Hi, Jerry," said Gerber. "You going to brief us on this?"

Maxwell shook his head. "I'm here to provide an intelligence update on the topic."

"Which is?" asked Fetterman.

"Nope, can't tell you."

"But we're going to find out in a few minutes anyway," said Fetterman.

Gerber didn't wait for a response. "You the one who asked for us on this?"

"Nope," said Maxwell. "That came down from on high. Seems you two have been involved in so many important missions, all with a certain degree of success, that you just naturally get mentioned whenever someone thinks up a new important mission."

"Great!" said Fetterman. "That's what you get for being good. All the shit missions. Maybe we should fuck up a couple and then we'd be forgotten."

Maxwell touched the leather folder he carried. "I'll see the two of you inside."

The CIA man turned and entered the building. Gerber watched him and then said, "You might be right, Tony, maybe we should fuck up a couple of them." He shrugged once. "Guess we better get going, too."

Together they walked across the grass to the door. Fetterman opened it and Gerber stepped in. There was a short hallway in front of him; the floor was dirty plywood. Off to one side was a small dayroom with two men sitting in it watching a tiny black-and-white television. Neither of them looked up as the door opened.

Gerber moved down the hall and then stopped outside a door. He hesitated before opening it but finally did. He entered, then stepped aside so that Fetterman could get in.

Before him was a table surrounded by chairs. On another, much smaller table, off to one side, sat a slide projector, the fan running to keep it cool. A screen had been erected in one corner. On the walls were the standard Army lithographs of soldiers fighting everyone from the Sioux to the North Koreans. Overhead a fan turned, but the room was sealed off so that it could be air-conditioned.

Maxwell gestured at a couple of chairs. "Why don't you two sit down?"

Gerber did, but Fetterman remained standing. He had his back to the wall, as if ready to run out if the chance presented itself.

"Let's see," said Maxwell, "you already know Major Jorgenson and Sergeant Teppler."

Gerber nodded at Jorgenson. A small wiry man who looked younger than he was, he had light hair and a thin face and wore fatigues that looked as if they had just been issued. They were bright green and bore only a bright gold oak leaf on one side of his collar and the crossed rifles of the infantry on the other.

Teppler was an older man. His hair had been cut short so that it bristled on his head like a scrub brush. His round face was reddish, but not from the sun. It seemed more likely that Teppler spent a good deal of his time hanging around clubs drinking beer. Like Jorgenson, he wore brand-new fatigues, but without any insignia on them.

"Last," said Maxwell, "is Colonel Johnson. He's in command of a fighter wing and has a few problems that we might be able to solve for him."

Gerber glanced at the man who wore a one-piece Nomex flight suit. He didn't bother to look up or acknowledge Gerber in any way.

Maxwell leaned over and flipped a switch on the back of the projector. "Get the lights, will you, Tony?" When it was dark and the first slide was in position, Maxwell said, "This is the railroad and highway bridge at Thanh Hoa, about seventy miles south of Hanoi."

"What's that have to do with us?" asked Fetterman, finally slipping into a chair.

"You'll see in a moment."

PHILLIPS STOOD outside the station manager's office, smoking cigarette after cigarette. It was dark in the lobby, the only light coming from a single lamp on a low table near the couch. Travis sat on the couch, his feet on the coffee table in front of him, his head against the wall and his eyes closed.

"How can you be so relaxed?" demanded Phillips.

He opened his eyes and looked at her. "Won't do any good to get upset about it. Either we'll get the money and approval to go, or we won't."

Phillips moved toward him, bent down and put out her cigarette. In a hushed voice she asked, "You know what this story means? Really means? Possible network feed and exposure. Careers have been built on less than that. We come back with a good story, come back with something controversial, and we'll be able to write our own ticket out of here."

Travis looked at the door, which remained closed. On either side of it were glass panels, but there were curtains over those panels so that they couldn't see into the office. They could tell there was a light on, and once they had heard voices, but they had no idea what was happening.

Phillips sat down next to Travis and faced him. Her knees were inches from his thigh. He was suddenly aware that she was a good-looking woman—ambitious, ruthless, competent and good-looking. He pushed the thought from his mind.

"I don't know about you," Phillips said, "but I don't want to be stuck here at a second-rate TV station for the rest of my life, covering the local bake-off and driving out into the country to talk with the farmer who went weird and painted everything lime green. I really don't care that the local PTA is raising money for a new playground or that the mayor has decided to raise the parking meter rate. There are important stories to be covered, and this is our one chance to show we're capable of covering them."

Travis shook his head. "My dear, there's nothing to worry about now. Just sit there and relax until they make a decision."

"They're deciding about my life, my career. Some asshole with a bean-counter mentality is going to decide whether it's worth the money to send a reporter to Hanoi. If he says no, then my career ends."

"You mean you'd quit?"

"No, stupid, but I won't get another chance like this. The goddamn networks are going to fall all over themselves to get their hands on reports from Hanoi."

Before Travis could reply the door opened and Chapman waved to them. Phillips was on her feet and moving toward the door before Chapman could invite them in.

"Have a seat," said Chapman, gesturing at the conference area in one corner of the room. There were four plush chairs and a couch around a low, square table that held a tray containing a wine decanter and half a dozen glasses. Floor-to-ceiling bookcases lined one wall and a huge color television, tuned to their own station squatted in another corner. A massive rosewood desk and a judge's chair, completing the furniture, sat in front of a wall of windows that looked out onto San Francisco.

"Well?" asked Phillips as she sat down.

Chapman turned toward the station manager, a short rotund man with thinning hair. He had a pudgy face and even in the air-conditioned office he was sweating.

Chapman gestured at the man. "Mr. Blodgett and I have spent the past few minutes going over the planned budget and the possible benefits to the station."

"And?" asked Phillips, sitting on the edge of her chair.

Finally Chapman smiled. "Though it might strain the news budget in other directions, we feel this is an opportunity too good to pass up."

"All right!" shouted Phillips. "All right!" Then she remembered where she was and added, "That's great."

Blodgett collapsed into a chair opposite them and stared at Phillips. "I want to make one thing clear. This is going to be no-frills. I'm not completely convinced this is a story we need to cover. The networks are better equipped for it."

"Why?" asked Phillips, speaking without thinking.

"Why?" echoed Blodgett. "Because, young lady, they have the people experienced in this sort of thing. They're trained to look below the surface and ferret out the story under the story."

Phillips felt her blood boil. She stared at the station manager, telling herself it wouldn't do any good to get into a shouting match with the man who signed her paychecks. But the words came tumbling out anyway. "Those people at the networks are no better than me. We've all had the same training, doing the same things. They all started in the same places, working for small-minded men who couldn't see beyond their own financial statements. I can do as good a job as anyone you could name at any one of the networks. The only difference between them and me is that they have bosses who respect their talent."

"Carla," snapped Chapman.

"No," said Blodgett. "Listen, if you feel that way, maybe you'd just better clean your desk and get out of here. You'd probably feel better working in a different environment."

The color drained from Phillips's face, and she looked as if she was about to pass out. She fell back in her chair, unable to speak.

Travis stood up. "Wait a minute. Mr. Blodgett, you'll have to forgive Carla. She's very sensitive about her work, and you have to admit that you called her second-rate."

"I did no such thing," said Blodgett.

Travis waved a hand. "Not in so many words, but you implied that our work here is somehow second-rate when compared to the work done at the networks. That's just not true. Given the time, and more importantly, given the money, we can produce work that's as good as, if not better than, anything you'll see at the networks."

"Now I never meant—" Blodgett began.

"No, sir, I know you didn't. Carla just jumped to conclusions. I'm sure she'll apologize." Travis looked at her. "You are sorry, aren't you, Carla?"

She sat forward again, some of the color back in her face. "Of course. Of course. But you have to understand how I feel. I work damn hard to turn out a quality program without the resources of the networks. This is my chance to prove we can do it all as well as the networks."

Chapman stepped forward then and said, "You know how high-strung these creative people can get. Sometimes they don't realize what they're saying."

Blodgett pulled a huge handkerchief from his pocket and mopped his face with it. "I understand that, but they have to see it from my side as well. We're not a money machine like the networks. We're taking a big risk here, and I think a certain amount of appreciation should be shown."

"We do appreciate the opportunity," Travis said hastily.

"And you, young lady?" asked Blodgett.

"Of course I do. This is a marvelous opportunity, not only for me, but for the station, as well."

Blodgett nodded. "All right, then, that's cleared up. Now, has anyone thought about the timing for this great excursion?"

"Now that we have approval," Chapman said, "and have a budget in mind, we'll contact the various people at the embassies and in the State Department to get the visas and passports arranged."

"I'll want to see a schedule by the end of the week."

"That shouldn't be a problem."

AS SOON AS MAXWELL began showing his slides, Gerber knew what was coming. It was like a poorly plotted movie where everyone in the theater knew what was going to happen. Maxwell didn't have any sense of drama or a flair for suspense. He just threw up the slides of the Thanh Hoa bridge, talked about the Air Force failure to do more than drop a span or two and then moved on, talking about the traffic that crossed the bridge on a daily basis.

Before Maxwell could continue, Fetterman asked, "Why is the Air Force having a problem taking out the bridge?"

"Let's hold the questions until the end," said Maxwell.

"No," said Johnson, "I'd like to tackle that one now, if you don't mind."

"Go right ahead." Maxwell sat down, leaving the black-and-white grainy photo of the bridge on the screen.

Johnson stood up and moved forward. He stopped in front of the screen so that the picture of the bridge was displayed on his chest and face.

"Our major problem is that the enemy, knowing this is a prime target, has erected a wide range of air defense around the bridge site. This includes everything from 12.7 mm machine guns up to SAM Twos. They've installed the ZSU-23/4, a multibarreled weapon with a radar-guidance system, and anytime a pilot flies a straight course for more than three to five seconds, a radar lock can be made. The problem, then, is that we can't line up as we would on the range, fly in straight and drop our bombs."

Johnson turned and stepped aside. "As you can see, if we come in from the west or the east, we have a small target. A bomb long or short will fall harmlessly into the river. Once the bomb is released, we have no control over it, so that all kinds of outside factors take over, making it very hard to hit the bridge at all."

With one hand Johnson indicated the clusters of buildings, trucks and sandbagged structures on the approach paths to the bridge. "The North Vietnamese, knowing that we've got to fly in on the long axis, have concentrated their defenses there. We're forced to dodge and weave as we go in. Those stresses also affect the bombs, making it hard to hit the bridge. Our success rate hasn't been all that great."

Maxwell took over again. "Thank you, Bruce." The slide changed. "Here we have the latest result of our attempts to knock down the bridge. This was taken three days ago, just after the last raid. As you can see, we only got one span."

The slide changed again. "And this was taken yesterday by a high-flying recon plane." Maxwell let the silence grow for a moment and then switched off the projector. "Lights," he said.

Fetterman switched them on and returned to his seat.

"Now," said Maxwell, "there's a new factor added." He glanced at Johnson. "The order will be coming down the pipe soon. The President's going to order a bombing halt in an attempt to bring the North Vietnamese to the conference table."

"That doesn't make sense," said Gerber.

"He's not trying to beat them into submission, but trying to entice them to come. Bargain in good faith."

"Shit," said Johnson. "That knocks us out of the picture completely."

"Not necessarily. The President's taken Hanoi targets off the list, but he's still going to allow us to hit targets north of the DMZ where the North Vietnamese are building up troop and equipment concentrations."

"So what does all this mean?" asked Jorgenson.

"It means we're going to put a ground team in to blow up the bridge. It means we're going to take out not only the spans, but the abutments, too. If we destroy those, it'll take the North Vietnamese months, maybe a couple of years, to repair the bridge." He looked at Johnson. "Given the President's restrictions, we believe the Thanh Hoa bridge still falls on the acceptable list. To cover the ground team, we'll want an air strike in there, as well."

"When do we start planning this?" asked Fetterman.

Maxwell picked up a briefcase. "Now, if there are no objections, we need a preliminary study done so that we can set the wheels in motion."

He passed out folders, each covered with bright red Secret stamps. When each man had one, Maxwell said, "Now, I know that all of you have come in here cold, so I don't expect much today."

Gerber opened the folder and found a series of aerial photos of the bridge. He studied them closely, seeing the large number of defensive positions around it. There were gun emplacements for light weapons, heavy weapons and at least two SAM sites, one within half a klick of the south side and the other no more than a klick to the north. There were also optically sighted ZSU-23s and the radar-controlled weapons. "I don't see anything here for ground defense."

"No," agreed Maxwell. "The North Vietnamese aren't worried about any kind of ground assault. They know the effort is going to be directed at them from the air."

"That's something," said Gerber.

Fetterman flipped through the material quickly. "These all the pictures we have?"

"What's wrong with them?" asked Johnson.

Fetterman looked at the officer. "From an air strike standpoint, probably nothing. Everything you need to know about the bridge is there, but if we're going in to do the job on the ground, there are lots of things I need to know. I can't even see the structure of the abutments from these, let alone the thickness of the steel in the spans. I can't begin to guess how to wire the bridge without more detailed information."

"What would you like to have, Master Sergeant?" Maxwell asked.

"If I could get my wish granted, I'd like the blueprints and specifications for the bridge. I'd like to know the formula for mixing the concrete and how it was reinforced. I'd like to know where the steel was forged and the process used to forge it. With that information I could tell you exactly how to drop the whole thing into the river."

"Failing that?" asked Maxwell.

"Better pictures of the structure. These aren't adequate."

"I'm afraid there are no ground-level pictures available," said Maxwell.

"Fine," said Fetterman. "That's typical. Everyone wants us to do a job, but no one has the information we need to do it."

"If that's such a problem," said Johnson, "why don't you just go look at it yourself?"

Fetterman pulled the map from the package, noted the location of the bridge, then looked at Gerber.

"I don't know about that, Tony."

"Piece of cake, Captain. We could swim ashore, walk to the bridge in a day and then walk back out. Hell, we wouldn't even have to carry food if we didn't want to."

Gerber rubbed a hand over his face and studied the map. He looked at pictures of the bridge and then the surrounding countryside. To Maxwell he said, "If we were going to do this right, Colonel Johnson has a point. We should go in and take a look at the structure so that we're not relying on photos and interpretations that might not be everything we need."

"Won't that tip your hand?" asked Johnson, surprised they'd take his suggestion seriously.

"Not if we do it right. Sneak in, look around, sneak out. No reason for them to even know we've been there," said Fetterman.

"And if Major Jorgenson starts selecting a Commando team now, we can get the ball rolling that much faster," Gerber added.

Maxwell looked at the men in the room. "Anything else?"

"We can't really plan much more until we've got the intelligence we need," Gerber said.

"How soon would you go?" asked Johnson.

"We'll figure that out after a little more work," said Gerber.

"All right, then," said Maxwell, "I suggest we adjourn. Major Jorgenson, I'll want to see you in my office tomorrow morning about ten. Gerber, you and Fetterman better return to MACV with me."

"And what about the Air Force?" asked Johnson.

"Right now there isn't much for you to do."

"We'll need to coordinate our activities later," said Gerber.

"Later. It's always later."

"Hell, sir," said Fetterman, "it's better than having to walk in to look at the bridge."

Johnson nodded, but didn't say a word.

3

CARRIAGE AND GASLITE
APARTMENTS
SAN FRANCISCO

The bedroom was a shambles. Carla Phillips had pulled out every article of clothing she owned and had spread them on the bed, on the chair in the corner or on the floor. A large suitcase sat at the end of the bed, but she hadn't put anything into it. She was trying to decide what she had to take, what she wanted to take and what she had to leave behind.

After she had left the budget meeting with Blodgett, she had rushed home, taken off her dress and then, in only her panties and bra, had started to pack. Now, after thirty minutes, she hadn't packed a thing.

On television the correspondents in South Vietnam all dressed for the part. Some wore khaki bush jackets that had big loops on the chests to hold large-caliber bullets in the fashion of Saturday matinee great white hunters. Others wore jungle fatigues that had no insignia on them, almost as if they were soldiers in a secret army. Neither costume seemed right for Phillips. She needed something else, something that would establish her image for the networks when she finally sent them films of her work in North Vietnam. The problem was that she hadn't figured out what that image should be.

Thoughts had come and gone. She considered copying the bush jacket style, including a knee-length skirt and black boots. She'd thought about jungle fatigues, but no one looked good in them except big men. Because she was going to be in North Vietnam, a poor country that wasted its gross national product in a war, she thought about the simple, drab jackets the Chinese were fond of. But then she remembered that the Chinese and the Vietnamese were enemies, and had been for about a thousand years. That shot down the Chinese idea.

The image she projected from the streets of Hanoi was almost as important as the stories she reported. The wrong image would destroy her faster than a bad story. Journalists realized that everyone got a clunker once in a while, but a bad image was something that could take years to wipe away. The choice had to be right.

She pushed the clothes off the chair and sat down, looking at the chaos around her. A dark blazer and dark pants. Maybe a light-colored blouse. That seemed to be the ticket. And boots so she could hike through the roughest terrain.

"Yeah," she said out loud. It made sense and it would look good on camera.

Suddenly there was a knock on the door. She snatched a robe from the pile of clothes and put it on as she walked to the door. Using the peephole, she looked out at the distorted face of Richard Travis.

"Just a second," she called.

She unlocked the door and opened it as she turned to retreat to the living room/dining area of the small apartment. Travis didn't say a word. He headed directly to the refrigerator and took out a can of beer.

"You want one?"

"No. What are you doing here?"

Travis walked into the living room and looked at the litter there. Books, magazines, newspapers were everywhere. There was a pizza box on the coffee table with most of the pizza gone. The ashtrays were overflowing. On the TV was a lava light that held a huge red blob throbbing in golden liquid.

Travis pushed a pile of books onto the floor. He noted that Phillips's reading wasn't confined to nonfiction. She had a number of science fiction novels in the pile. One or two of them piqued his interest: they had scantily clad women on the covers.

"I'm here," said Travis, "because I thought we should coordinate this trip a little better. Talk about it here without having to worry about people overhearing us."

Phillips nodded and then leaned forward to snatch her cigarettes from the table. Her left hand clutched at her robe, holding it tightly together so that Travis couldn't see anything. As she lit a cigarette, she asked, "So what's on your mind?"

"Okay," said Travis. He took a long pull on his beer. "You have any idea what we're going to look for on this story?"

"That all that's bothering you? Hell, that's simple. We look for evidence that the Administration's lying when it says only military targets are being bombed. We go to Hanoi and film the North Vietnamese going about their daily lives as they wait for death to rain down on them. We show women and children cowering in terror as the bombs fall, killing indiscriminately."

"And if that's not what we see?"

"Hell, Dick, that's exactly what we're going to see. First, the North Vietnamese wouldn't be inviting in journalists if that wasn't what we'd see. Second, I can't believe we're so good, meaning our pilots are so well trained, that a few of the bombs don't hit civilian targets. We're just going to tell the story from the perspective of the people on the ground."

"We're not going to talk to our Air Force about it?"

Phillips leaned forward to tap her cigarette on the ashtray. She had forgotten about her robe, and let it fall open briefly. Travis got a flash of breast as she straightened.

"Why ask our Air Force? We know what the answer's going to be. Hell, we've got stock footage of their responses that we can cut into anything new we get. They're going to say they don't hit civilian targets, though sometimes the bombs fall short, or long, and some damage to noncombatant areas is unavoidable. Christ, I love that. Noncombatant, meaning civilians."

Travis leaned back in his chair and closed his eyes. He held the beer can high, almost as if it were some kind of religious symbol.

"How soon do you think we can get to North Vietnam?" asked Phillips.

"Guessing, I'd say the paperwork will get through the North Vietnamese end of it in a couple of days at most. They want us to come. The State Department might drag its feet, though a simple TV report saying they're inhibiting the flow of news would be enough to get them moving. A week?"

"Shit. I thought we'd be out of here faster than that."

Travis grinned. "You know there are no direct flights from here to Hanoi. We've got to go to Europe. I thought we'd have to fly out of Moscow but Sweden, among other places, has flights to Hanoi."

"Hadn't thought of that."

"I put a couple of people on it, getting them to arrange the flights to Hanoi. Once we're there I guess they'll show us around."

"As you can see, I've been busy packing."

"That's a good idea," said Travis. "Things could break so that we need to move in a matter of hours." He watched as she crossed her legs and her robe parted, revealing her thighs. She seemed not to notice.

Travis drained the rest of his beer. "Well, I suppose I better get going." He didn't make a move to leave.

Phillips butted her cigarette in the ashtray, stood up and looked down at him. "I want to thank you for helping sell this to the big bosses. I don't think they'd have let me beat them into it if they didn't trust you."

"It's going to be a hell of a story," he said, standing.

As she moved toward the door, she stopped and said, "It's nice to be working with you again. It's been a long time since we worked closely."

Travis reached the door. "Yes. A long time."

GERBER AND FETTERMAN were enjoying the coolness of Jerry Maxwell's office. It was in the basement of MACV Headquarters, hidden behind an iron gate guarded by a bored MP with an M-16.

Gerber sat in a big chair near Maxwell's battleship-gray desk, which was covered with a blizzard of paper and lined with empty Coke cans. Along the opposite wall of the office was a bank of filing cabinets, the last one a huge, thick thing with a combination lock on the second drawer. The tops of the filing cabinets were covered with more papers. Normally Fetterman stood there, leaning against the cabinets, but this time he sat on a metal folding chair.

Maxwell was behind his desk. He reached out, grabbed a Coke can, shook it once and determined there was nothing to drink in it. There never seemed to be any Coke in the cans. Finally the CIA man turned to face his guests. "Is this trip really necessary?"

Gerber shrugged. "Jerry, if you want us to destroy that bridge, then, yes, the trip is necessary. We have to see the structure before we can begin to figure out how to drop it. You just want all the spans in the water, then it's not that big a problem."

"How do you want to handle this?" Maxwell asked.

Gerber looked around. "You got a map?"

Maxwell dug through the papers on his desk and produced one. He spread it out. "Okay?"

"Two ways of doing this. We swim in, hike through the jungle and spy on the bridge, or we parachute in."

"Captain," said Fetterman, "we parachute into the river and then float downstream, it's going to be a lot easier on us. Once we've seen the bridge, we work our way around and then float toward the ocean."

"Could we get a chopper in to pick us up?" Gerber asked.

Maxwell shrugged. "That shouldn't be a problem. Hell, ten, twelve klicks into North Vietnam is a piece of cake. The search-and-rescue boys have tried to get to men near Hanoi and have had some success."

"Then we've got it made," Gerber said.

"How long would this take?" Maxwell asked.

Gerber glanced at Fetterman. "Hell, drop in about dawn, see the bridge and be ready for extraction by noon. Won't take long at all."

"Sergeant?" asked Maxwell.

"The captain's right. We just have to see the abutments and the steel under the surface of the road. Once we've seen that, we can get out. Until we've seen it, there's no good way to determine what we need to drop the bridge."

"When would you like to leave?"

Gerber looked at his watch and then at Maxwell. "I would think we'd want to hit the water day after tomorrow. Gives us time to get the equipment and uniforms together and for you to coordinate the air assets we're going to need. Oh, one other thing. Maybe we should use Air Force parachutes, if you can get them."

"Why's that?"

"Going into the river we'll want to drop out of the harness early which will make it easier on us. We won't have to recover the chutes, because if the North Vietnamese find them, they won't think about a covert mission. They'll figure there are a couple of downed airmen around."

"That's simple enough. Anything else?"

"Just one thing," Gerber said, smiling. "Robin gets back from Japan day after tomorrow. Get us reservations for dinner, will you?"

"You'll be back by then?"

"Shit, we should be back in time to meet her at the airport."

"Shows how lucky some civilians can be," said Maxwell. "Getting out of this hellhole once in a while has to be good for the soul. No worries about the enemy dropping a mortar on you or getting caught in a cross fire."

"Well," said Fetterman, "if there's nothing else, we've got some work to do."

"Fine. You'll need to meet with me once more before you go."

"I'll call you tomorrow," Gerber said, "to arrange for the meeting." He stood.

"Tomorrow, then."

Gerber and Fetterman had been gone for only a few minutes when there was a knock at Maxwell's door. He looked toward it and yelled, "Come on in."

A short balding man in stained khaki entered. His chubby face had a ruddy complexion and he was sweating heavily. After he entered, he closed the door and leaned against it, breathing heavily, as if he had run all the way to Maxwell's office. Maxwell didn't know much about the man who'd arrived from Washington only a couple of weeks earlier. All he really knew was that Pat had the juice to get anything he wanted. That was not something anyone could do. "How'd it go?" he asked.

Maxwell stared at him. "Everyone came on board just as they should have, Pat."

Pat moved to the chair that Gerber had used and dropped into it. "You had no trouble convincing them of the value of the bridge?"

"That was the least of the problems. Everyone was ready to hit it right away. The ground pounders said they'd have to make a personal recon before they could be sure they knew enough to destroy it."

Pat took a damp handkerchief from his pocket and wiped his face with it; all he did was rearrange the sweat. "This recon a good idea?"

"Knowing Gerber and Fetterman, they wouldn't go into the operation without it."

"What about the Air Force?"

"Johnson wasn't happy when we put the emphasis on the ground operation, but he'll take his role. Keeps his men from getting killed."

Pat nodded. "I think that if we can get that bridge knocked out for more than a couple of days, the President will be very happy. Gives him an extra bargaining chip when they finally get to the peace table."

"Seems to me there should be an easier way of doing this."

"You don't worry about it, Jerry. You just get that damned bridge destroyed and everyone'll be happy."

"Yes, sir."

GERBER AND FETTERMAN flagged a taxi as they left the MACV compound, and ordered the driver to take them downtown. As they climbed into the rear of the battered, multicolored Chevy, Gerber thought that things were getting strange again.

War should be fought by two armies in bright uniforms in open fields where the civilians couldn't be injured. For centuries that was what had happened. The Battle of Gettysburg had been fought in Pennsylvania over three days, and when it was over only one civilian had been killed.

But war had changed. Civilians in the cities were now the hostages of the combatants. Kill enough of the civilian population, destroy enough of the civilian areas, and one side gave up. In Vietnam it was now a question of destroying a village to save it.

As they started downtown, Fetterman interrupted Gerber's train of thought. "What's the plan for this evening?"

Gerber glanced at the driver and shrugged. "Dinner, I suppose."

"Nothing more pressing?"

"Anything we have to do can easily be accomplished tomorrow in just a few hours. That is, unless you've got something else in mind."

"No, sir. Just wondering."

Gerber fell silent and wondered why he was suddenly depressed. Maybe it was the thought of all those Air Force missions against the bridge that had turned out to be such a waste. No one had sat down to think through the whole thing. Just stuff the pilots into the jets and send them out. When that failed, find someone else and try it again.

They roared through the late-afternoon streets of Saigon. There was a riot of noise around them, caused by the jets overhead and the bars on the ground. Music blasted from everywhere, punctuated by the rumbling of diesel engines and the buzzing of Hondas and Lambrettas.

Sweat dripped down Gerber's face, and he reached over to roll down the window. The odors of Saigon blew in at him— a mixture of excrement, of partially burnt fuel, of mildew, of humidity. There was a hint of rain in the air.

But unlike other rides into the city, Gerber wasn't interested in looking around. He'd seen it all before, from the soldiers chasing women to the MPs and White Mice chasing soldiers. It was an artificial world created by the fighting. No matter how the war ended, the Saigon he knew would be gone with the last of the American troops.

They pulled out of the traffic and stopped in front of the Carasel Hotel. Gerber opened the door and slipped out, but Fetterman remained in the back, arguing with the driver about the fare. It didn't matter what the price was; Fetterman always had an argument. The master sergeant enjoyed the challenge of getting the driver to reduce his fare. He claimed he was doing his bit to hold down the local inflation rate.

When Fetterman joined him on the sidewalk, Gerber said, "I think I'll go up to my room."

"You feeling okay, Captain?"

"I'm fine. Tired."

Before either of them moved, Fetterman said, "Had a thought on the way over here. Maybe we should take Kit with us. Her knowledge of the local terrain might prove invaluable."

"I don't know, Tony. That seems like one complication we really don't need. In and out is the secret of success on this one."

"Just a thought, sir."

"Not much of one."

"Yes, sir. What about dinner?"

Gerber shrugged and looked at the entrance to the hotel. A large door, filled with glass and surrounded by black marble, it looked as if it should have been in New York or London, not in Saigon. It was strangely out of place. "Thought I'd skip it tonight."

"We should begin eating heavily."

Gerber knew what Fetterman was saying. You ate as much as possible until it was time for a mission. That way you only had to carry emergency rations into the jungle. He knew he should try to live off the food he'd eaten in the past two days, but a large meal didn't appeal to him right now. He was getting depressed and didn't know if it was because Robin Morrow was in Japan or because she was coming back. Once out of Vietnam, she should have made good her escape.

"You're right, Tony. We'll get together for dinner and eat everything in sight."

"Good, sir. Should I call for you?"

"No, I'll meet you down here in about an hour."

"Yes, sir."

With that Gerber opened the door and stepped into the hotel. As he crossed the lobby, he thought, What a hell of a way to fight a war.

4

MACV-SOG
TAN SON NHUT
SAIGON

Gerber stood outside in the early-morning mist and watched
the aircraft as they took off and landed. The lights, subdued
because of the threat of enemy mortars, were ringed with tiny
rainbows from the moisture in the air. Overhead, the moon
was little more than a dull smudge seen through the thin clouds
that hid the stars.

Gerber stepped back and leaned against the sandbags that
protected the lower four feet of the building. Inside, Fetterman was checking the parachutes that Maxwell had gotten
from the Air Force. He was checking the equipment they
would be carrying with them—weapons, ammo, canteens,
first-aid kits and LRRP rations.

After five minutes of watching the fighters and listening to
the roar of engines, Gerber needed a break. He opened the
door, moved down the hallway and entered the storeroom at
the far end of the building. It held racks of equipment, clothing, supplies and rations. Everything a man needed to outfit
a patrol could be found in the room. A covert operation into
Laos was no problem. The room contained fatigues from
Germany, rifles from Britain and maps from France. There

were dozens of items made in every country in the world, including firearms from behind the iron curtain. Someone had spent the better part of his tour organizing and acquiring the gear.

Gerber moved to one of the long tables and sat down on the folding chair there. The captain watched as Fetterman checked the parachutes; obviously he didn't trust the Air Force riggers. Satisfied with that, the master sergeant moved to the next pile of equipment and began inspecting it. Gerber had gone over it earlier, making sure everything was in working order and that it was all there, but Fetterman wanted to double-check.

"I think we're in good shape," said Gerber.

"Yes, sir."

But the master sergeant didn't stop his inspection. Once, when Gerber had asked Fetterman why he was so cautious, he had pointed out that he would be using the equipment, too. He didn't like leaving anything in the hands of someone who wouldn't be going on the mission. When Gerber had pointed out that he, too, was going, Fetterman had shrugged and said, "I've been doing it for so long it's second nature now." Gerber knew that the rule was to check everything as often as possible so that the equipment didn't let you down when you needed it most.

"Satisfied?" asked Gerber when Fetterman finally sat down.

"Yes, sir. Everything's here and looks good."

Gerber glanced at his watch. "We've got about twenty minutes before the jeep arrives."

Fetterman stood and began to divide the equipment so that there was a pile for each of them, while Gerber began packing his share into a rucksack. Because it was a short-range mission that was supposed to last less than a day, there wasn't that much to take. Within five minutes Gerber had his rucksack packed and on his back.

Just then, Maxwell appeared at the door. He stopped and shook his head slowly, as if unsure of what to do. "You boys about ready?"

"We're all set, Jerry. And good morning to you, too," Gerber quipped.

"I've got the jeep standing by," the CIA man told them.

Gerber shouldered one of the parachute harnesses and waited as Fetterman picked up the other. He then reached down and grabbed his weapon and a bandolier of ammo for it.

With Maxwell in the lead, they walked out of the building and into the night. Gerber dropped the parachute into the back of the jeep and then climbed into the passenger seat. Fetterman dropped his gear on top of Gerber's and jumped in after it. Maxwell slipped behind the wheel and started the engine. It backfired once, and the CIA man ground the gears trying to find first.

"Keep grinding," said Fetterman. "They'll fit eventually."

Maxwell finally got the vehicle going and headed in the direction of the Air America pad, which was over by Hotel Three. Sitting on the pad were four silver C-47s. Maxwell pulled up beside one and stopped.

"Everything's arranged now. Fighters are going in at about dawn to drop a few bombs. They're just going to blow up some worthless real estate so the President can claim the bombing halt is still in effect."

"Maybe it would be better to forget about that. Might tip our hand," Gerber said.

Maxwell peered at the captain. "Thought of that myself, but I decided that any mission, no matter what was hit, would tend to cover your infiltration. The North Vietnamese will just figure the fighters punched off the bombs over empty terrain, as they sometimes do."

Fetterman turned and saw a single plane sitting off by itself. He could just make out its silhouette. The camouflage was dark in order to make the plane difficult to see at night. "That our ride?"

"Right," said Maxwell. "Get your gear over to it and I'll try to round up the crew."

Gerber reached out and grabbed Maxwell's arm. "This mean we don't have an Air Force crew?"

"Nope. CIA."

"Shit."

Maxwell stared hard at Gerber. "Got a problem with that?"

"At least with the Air Force we'd get a professional crew interested in putting us down in the right spot. With the CIA no one knows what's going on. Our mission might just be a cover for another mission, just as the bombing mission is a cover for us."

"This is the priority mission. The crew has one job, and that's to get the two of you into North Vietnam."

"I wish you'd quit saying that out loud around here," Fetterman snapped.

"There's no one listening."

"And there weren't no Indians at Little Bighorn, neither."

"Let's go," said Gerber. He got out of the jeep and moved behind it.

"You wait here and I'll check on the status of the crew," Maxwell said.

"They damn well better have arrived and started the preflight, or we're not going to be leaving here on time," Gerber groused.

"You worry about your end of it," Maxwell said, "and I'll worry about mine."

"Yes, sir, Mr. Maxwell, sir," Gerber cracked.

CARLA PHILLIPS SAT in her tiny station office. Not much larger than a closet, it held her desk, a typing table and a bookcase filled with volumes of nonfiction whose subjects ranged from the American Civil War to UFOs. Sitting on the floor, shoved against the wall so that it would be out of the way, was her suitcase. Next to it was a smaller case that held underwear, soap and two bottles of pills. She was ready to go just as soon as the word filtered down.

Chapman stuck his head in the doorway, one hand on the knob and the other on the wall, and asked, "What are you working on?"

"At the moment, not a thing. My assignment is to cover an attempt by four students to break a Guinness world record, but there won't be anything going on that until about three."

"Shelve it. I'll give it to someone else."

Phillips dropped her pencil onto the desktop. "We get it?"

"Car will be ready in about ten minutes. Camera crew is already taking their gear out to it. Papers are ready. Visas are ready. The State Department didn't drag its feet, but they cautioned us against sending anyone, given the current level of hostilities. Still, they didn't deny us the paperwork."

"Hot damn!"

Chapman pointed at the papers sitting on Phillips's desk. "Make a list of everything that can't wait for two weeks—the stories you're working on, things that will be coming up and any personal item that has to be taken care of."

"Got it."

"Leave it with me before you go." Chapman disappeared.

Phillips's mind raced. There were a hundred different things that should be done. Her laundry was at the cleaner's and had to be picked up. Her mother needed a birthday card. There were stories and ideas for stories that couldn't wait.

She tried to list everything in logical order, but that was impossible. Finally, in frustration, she listed items as they came to mind. When she was done, she placed the list in the center of her desk and put a heavy metallic paperweight, in the shape of a peace symbol, on top of it.

She got up, grabbed her purse and looked inside to see if her passport was in it. That was the last thing she wanted to forget. Satisfied that she had it, she checked to make sure she had a company credit card, some cash and some traveler's checks.

That finished, she shouldered the bag, picked up her suitcase and overnight case and headed out the door. There was no one in the hallway for her to say goodbye to. She stopped at Chapman's office, but he was gone. On her way to the garage she saw no one.

Chapman was standing at the rear of a station wagon filled with camera equipment, film, sound gear, lights and batteries. There were a couple of suitcases jammed in there and several more roped to the top of the car. Chapman was talking to Travis and two other men. They were young, dressed in sweatshirts and jeans, and looked more like war protesters than professional journalists. Tim Young was the cameraman and Paul Angstadt the sound man.

As Phillips approached, Chapman came toward her and took her suitcase. "I don't know what advice to give you on this one. It's the first time a reporter has gone to the enemy's capital in time of war."

"We're not at war with North Vietnam," she said.

"Good point. However, we are fighting them." Chapman shrugged and groped for words. "There should be something for me to tell you, but I'm damned if I can figure it out. Don't do anything to offend your hosts. I mean, remember where you are. Be careful."

When they reached the rear of the car, Phillips set her overnight case down. As she straightened up, she smiled. "I think I'm smart enough not to get off the plane and begin filming at the airport. I understand that we're guests and that the North Vietnamese can revoke our press credentials at any moment."

"Right," said Chapman. He turned to face the other men. "Now, as producer, Dick will be in command." He glanced at Phillips and added, "But Carla here has the authority to make decisions on the content of the film. Listen to her. But most of all, don't do anything stupid and piss off the North Vietnamese."

Tim grinned. "Right, boss. I'm just going to take pictures."

Chapman watched as Phillips's suitcase was put into the car. When the cameraman got her overnight case jammed in, he said, "That's got it."

Chapman nodded. "Now, Tim, Paul, remember, you're there to record the event. And, everyone, be fucking careful on this. I don't want to read about anyone being arrested and thrown in jail. There won't be much I can do for you if that happens."

"We've gone over this already," Travis complained.

"Right," Chapman said. "I'll just wish you all good luck, then. God, I wish I was going with you."

"Thanks," said Travis. "Tim, why don't you drive?"

"Oh, no," said Chapman. "I'll drive. We don't want the car sitting at the airport for two, three weeks."

"Then we're ready," said Travis.

They climbed into the car. Chapman started the engine, and one of the mechanics ran out and punched a button. The door rose, revealing the late-afternoon sun.

Phillips turned in her seat and watched as the garage door came down once they were outside. She suddenly felt alive, happy, the excitement bubbling through her. She couldn't resist saying, "This is it."

"IT'S ALL SET," Maxwell said. "The crew's aboard."

Gerber glanced at the plane, still not much more than a dark shape outlined by the airfield lights. "This the only mission for that plane today?"

"Come on, Mack, you're worrying about nothing. We needed a plane with a certain paint scheme, and the only one available was this one. The Air Force planes have a light gray belly that makes them easier to see at dawn."

"I don't like it," said Gerber.

Fetterman hadn't spoken during the exchange. Instead, he picked up his gear and headed for the aircraft. A door, just aft of the cockpit, had come open and the red light from the interior was bleeding onto the ramp.

"See," said Maxwell. "Sergeant Fetterman isn't worried about it."

"Sergeant Fetterman is currently so pissed off he won't talk to you. Neither of us likes this."

"All right, Captain," said Maxwell. "Orders can be issued."

"Not by you, Jerry. You can stand there and order all day long and I can call Nha Trang and Fifth Group is going to back me."

"You refusing to go?"

Gerber frowned. "No. I'm just registering a major protest concerning the equipment being employed."

"Protest noted," said Maxwell.

Gerber shook his head, then picked up his weapon and gear. Turning around, he walked toward the aircraft, stopped, glanced back over his shoulder, then continued on. He caught Fetterman at the hatch.

"You're not going to like this, Captain."

Gerber looked up into the cockpit. He could see three civilians sitting there. Or rather, he saw three men in civilian clothes. One was in the pilot's seat and two were on the long bench seat shoved against the bulkhead. He'd expected the pilots to be in civilian clothes. Hell, they were probably Air Force pilots flying for the CIA now.

"Not them," said Fetterman. He climbed up into the rear of the plane.

Gerber followed him and saw a huge wooden crate, the stenciling painted over so that it couldn't be read. Then, in the troop seats that lined one side of the fuselage, he saw a group of men dressed like an A-team. Each wore a green beret, jungle fatigues with no insignia on them and brand-new boots. On the left sleeve of each man was a gold-and-black armband.

Gerber leaned close to Fetterman. "Jesus Christ in a sleigh."

As he spoke, another civilian, a large man who looked as if he was more than a little ticked off, came toward them. "Sir, let me take your gear."

Gerber was reluctant to let go of his equipment. He didn't want anyone touching it now that he was getting ready to drop into enemy territory.

"I need to get it stored so we can take off."

Gerber glanced at the men seated along the fuselage. "I'm not convinced I want to do this."

"Sir?"

Fetterman handed the man his parachute and rucksack. Happy, the man set them at the end of a pile of equipment and supplies in the center of the aircraft. Turning back to Gerber, he held out his hands. Reluctantly the captain surrendered his gear.

After the man added it to the pile, he said, "Please take a seat and belt yourself in."

Gerber took a deep breath and looked toward the front. The hatch there had been closed. Just then, one of the engines began to turn slowly, then faster and faster until it was roaring. The interior of the C-130 was stripped down, as it would have been in an Air Force plane: red troop seats, webbing for a backrest, no soundproofing and bare control cables. With one engine running, it was hard to talk, and then the second was cranked, making communication impossible.

Gerber moved to a seat on the side of the fuselage across from the A-team. As he belted himself in, he studied the men. There was something about them that bothered Gerber, but he couldn't put his finger on it.

The last two engines started and the civilian-dressed loadmaster worked his way among the soldiers, checking to see if they had all buckled their seat belts properly. When he finished, he disappeared into the front. A moment later the plane jerked once, stopped and then began to taxi.

Fetterman leaned close and yelled, "We got what? A couple of hours?"

"At the very least."

Fetterman nodded. He turned and looked at the twelve men across the aircraft from him. None of them moved or returned his stare. They all sat quietly, their eyes on the deck in front of them. Not one of them spoke or seemed at all interested in what was happening around him. "You notice anything about these guys?"

"You mean other than that they've all got new uniforms and new boots?" Gerber shook his head. "How far you figure they'll be able to walk before they've got bleeding blisters?"

"They're all wearing their berets wrong."

Gerber glanced at them again. The flash on their berets wasn't centered over the eye the way it was supposed to be. Then be noticed that almost every one of the berets looked as new as the uniforms. "That goddamned Maxwell sandbagged us."

"Yes, sir."

The plane stopped moving for a moment, and then the engines began to roar even louder, causing the aircraft to vibrate. A few minutes later, after racing down the runway, it lifted off.

The climb continued and the air in the plane got cool and then cold. As that happened, the engines quieted slightly and the plane leveled out.

"You think they're going to get in our way?" asked Fetterman.

"I don't know. Just look at them. I hope they're not going to be jumping into North Vietnam, or at least into the jungles."

"It's the OSS tradition," said Fetterman. "Jumping into Nazi-occupied France to fight the Germans. They think they can do it in North Vietnam."

"Shit," Gerber grumbled. "This really pisses me off. In and out in a morning, if those assholes don't fuck us up."

"Maybe they're on their way to Laos."

"No," said Gerber. "There would be no reason to expose them to fire over North Vietnam. That's got to be where they're going. We're flying cover for them."

He fell silent and stared at the men opposite him. He'd worked with a CIA man once who hadn't understood life in the jungle. The man had been used to city streets and firefights that lasted two minutes. In the jungle, with thousands of rounds being fired, he had lost it. The urban spy just couldn't understand the differences.

Now Gerber was sitting across from twelve city kids who might have gone through the jungle warfare school in Panama, or who might have missed it. They probably thought they were jumping into a forest like the ones in the World— nice, neat little clumps of trees filled with cute little animals. They wouldn't be ready for the jungle, for the snakes and insects and the heat and the humidity. Hell, the new fatigues and brand-new boots told him that. They'd be able to walk ten miles, maybe, before the boots would tear up their feet.

"Maybe they won't get in our way," said Fetterman.

"And maybe pigs can fly," said Gerber. He knew that if there was a way for these guys to fuck up the mission, they'd do it. "Shit," he said again.

5

Bruce Johnson kept his eyes moving from the instrument panel of his F-4C Phantom to the aircraft of his flight, trying to watch everything that was happening around him. He was packed into the front seat of the fighter with his survival gear, his parachutes tucked up under the ejection seat, his anti-G suit and his pistol. In the cramped quarters he could move his feet and hands, but not much else. As always his back hurt and his shoulders ached and he wished he was on the way back to Saigon. That was when he'd finally get some relief.

He watched as the last of the planes in his flight refueled. When the jet broke away from the KC-135 tanker that had flown all the way from Guam, Johnson glanced at the navigation chart strapped to the holder on his thigh. Of course, he really didn't need a map; he was going back to the Thanh Hoa bridge and had been there often enough that he could find it in his sleep.

"Flight's joined," came the voice of Brewster Four.

"Roger, rolling over," Johnson said as he touched the throttle and nudged the stick.

According to the clock, only a little more than thirty minutes remained before he was to begin the attack. This time their approach would follow the course of the Song Ma. They would fly west along the river and hit the bridge that way. The briefing officer had told them it didn't matter whether they hit the bridge or not, just so long as they kept the air defenses busy for fifteen or twenty minutes.

Johnson had asked about the attack altitude and had been told it didn't matter. Worried about the SA-2s, he had decided to hit the bridge under two thousand feet. That would negate the SAM missiles but would leave them wide open for the ZSU-23s, the optically guided, and radar-controlled guns.

"Doesn't matter," he had told the men. "We'll be coming from a direction that isn't heavily defended. Everything's geared to hit us coming from the north or south. Coming from the east will limit our exposure, and then only a few guns will be trained on us."

No one had thought much of the idea, especially when they were told it was just a cover mission. Fly into the face of the enemy, drop bombs but don't worry about damaging the bridge. Johnson had to admit it was better than the original plan, which was to drop the bombs in a rice paddy somewhere close to the bridge.

Seeing that they were early, Johnson began a slow turn to the right, taking the flight back out over the South China Sea. There was no sense in orbiting over North Vietnam where some wise-ass gunner could make a name for himself.

After flying outbound for five minutes, he turned again, heading toward the North Vietnamese coast. Now he was on time, and as he saw the coast coming at him, a faint, dark line against the gray sea, he felt sweat blossom on his face.

This was supposed to be a milk run, he told himself. Just fly over the enemy and drop bombs. No one was to get hurt because it was a diversion, but those always turned into the roughest missions. It was as if the gods had decided it was time to wake everyone up. Let them relax and then hit them with a new weapons system or incredibly thick antiaircraft fire.

As they approached the coast, Johnson began a slow letdown. There was no reason to hurry, because the coast was still twenty miles away. He got on the radio and told the pilots in his flight what he was doing, something that wasn't necessary. His men would follow him closely, and if he flew into the ground, he expected them to fly into the ground with him.

"About to go feet dry," he said, warning the men.

"Brewster Two, roger."

"Three, roger."

"Ditto Brewster Four."

He glanced up into the sky, which was still dark. There seemed to be a slight fading of the stars, telling him that dawn was approaching, but not enough for him to be sure. About the time they hit the bridge there would be a gray-and-pink band in the east, but that shouldn't hurt them. They would be approaching for the attack from the blackness of the jungle.

As they crossed the North Vietnamese coastline, Johnson reached for the panel to begin arming the weapons systems. He flipped the switches until the panel glowed with lights, telling him that everything was hot. He didn't have to issue an order over the radio; it was SOP to arm the weapons once they were over enemy territory.

Johnson glanced to the right and looked down. Below him was the silvery thread of the Song Ma—a wide river with a distinctive delta area. Rice farms were all around it, leaving the ground uncluttered by forest, jungle or buildings. There were the occasional black shapes of farmer's hootches and a black ribbon of highway, none of which interested him.

Using the river as a guide, he turned west and began streaking toward the bridge. Overhead there was nothing to see. The rendezvous with the transport plane was based strictly on time. He would never see it, and it wouldn't see him or his flight. He'd drop his bombs, roll out to the south and then turn back to the South China Sea. The transport would turn to the north and then to the east for its egress.

"Coming up on the IP" came the voice of the man in the back seat.

Johnson nodded, knowing that his backseater wouldn't see the gesture. Over the radio he said, "IP inbound."

Each of the other planes acknowledged the call, and as they did, Johnson felt the pucker factor increase. He gripped the stick tighter and felt his legs tense. His heart hammered and his breathing became rapid and shallow. Sweat dripped from his forehead and splashed into his eyes, burning them. He blinked rapidly, but kept his mind on the task at hand.

In the distance a stream of tracers climbed slowly into the sky—glowing green pin lights that seemed miles away. Nothing for him to worry about.

And then he could see the target. For a moment everything below him was peaceful, but then the world exploded as he began the run in.

CARLA PHILLIPS RELAXED in the wide, plush seat of the first-class section of the jet. The air-conditioning kept the plane cool, and she had already plugged in the earphones to listen to the music. There were files and books to read, but she ignored them all as she relaxed.

Travis was next to her, a drink in hand already. The two technicians, the cameraman and the sound man, had gotten the delicate equipment stored and then moved to their seats in the coach section. They didn't grumble about it, knowing that Phillips was the star and that Travis was their boss.

The plane filled up quickly as the stewardesses moved among the passengers, making sure each one was happy. Phillips removed the earphones and grinned at a stewardess. She asked for a bottle of beer and then turned so that she could look out the window.

For a moment the plane sat motionless while the jet engines whined. Then the cabin lights flashed once, and over the public-address system the captain told them they would be taxiing out for the takeoff. As the jet moved, Phillips touched

Travis on the shoulder. "I can't believe we're really on the way."

After an initial pause, the jet sped up, lifted and began its ascent. Out the window, the city of San Francisco sparkled and grew smaller. Phillips watched the display briefly and then turned to Travis. "Maybe we'd better get some work done."

"There's no hurry."

Phillips leaned back. "I guess not."

FOR A FEW MINUTES Gerber watched the fake A-team. No one moved. They all sat quietly, staring straight ahead, as if they didn't have a care in the world. The team leader didn't get them together to go over the mission again. He didn't quiz them on the mission. They just sat there and waited.

The team sergeant was the same way. He did absolutely nothing, just sat there and stared at the deck between his feet, as did everyone else. The weapons man didn't check the weapons and the commo sergeant didn't check the radio. They all sat there, riding in the back of the plane like passengers heading for a night in Las Vegas.

Finally Gerber took out his map, folded it so that the Thanh Hoa bridge was centered and checked out the terrain. The map indicated a river valley, which in some places was bordered by high cliffs and steep hills, while in other sections flat land was the rule. Both jungle and rice paddies were found close to the river. Fortunately the rice paddies were either farther inland or close to the South China Sea. As far as he could tell, jungle covered the territory from the DZ to the bridge. That would provide good concealment for them.

Leaning toward Fetterman, Gerber touched the map and then looked at the other men. They paid no attention to either Gerber or Fetterman. With their attention elsewhere, Gerber again traced the path of the river, resting his finger at a place where a hill sloped down to the water. From the elevation markings, the hill looked fairly gentle, though it was high. From the summit they should be able to see down into the valley and look out onto the bridge. It was the perfect place to study the scene before making the final attempt to get under the bridge.

Fetterman nodded, then pointed on the map to a bend in the Song Ma downriver from the bridge. That was the pickup point. If something happened to Gerber, then Fetterman would have to get to it himself.

Finished, Gerber refolded the map so that the target wasn't on top, a standard precaution in case something happened during bailout. If the enemy somehow found the map, the target wouldn't be highlighted. For the same reason, Fetterman and Gerber had memorized everything they needed to know about the mission. It didn't pay to have a written plan fall into enemy hands.

Satisfied with that, Gerber sat back and closed his eyes. He didn't look across the deck at the men in their brand-new fatigues and boots. He didn't want to know who they were or what they were doing. He just knew they weren't Special Forces men. Everything about them was wrong.

It seemed as if only a few minutes had passed when Fetterman touched him on the shoulder. Gerber opened his eyes and saw the master sergeant pointing at his watch. They were getting close.

Fetterman moved to the equipment and began checking it out. As he did, the loadmaster came forward and unfastened the cargo straps that had been laced through the harnesses.

Gerber got up and crouched next to Fetterman. Together they separated their equipment from the rest. Gerber donned his rucksack and pistol belt and then slipped into the bandoliers of spare ammo. He tucked a small URC-10 radio, grenades, spare magazines, a compass and the map into various pockets, then watched Fetterman do the same thing.

That finished, they checked each other and then put on the parachutes, snugging down the harnesses. As they worked, Gerber glanced at the bogus A-team, but no one seemed the least bit curious about them.

"You know any of those guys?" Gerber asked Fetterman.

"Never seen any of them before."

"Damn that Maxwell anyway. We should get his ass up here and let him worry about everything."

The loadmaster approached them again. He stooped and secured the cables that had loosened when Fetterman and Gerber had extracted their equipment. When he finished, he turned to Gerber. "We're about ten minutes out."

They all moved to the rear troop door. The loadmaster stood there for a few moments, looking out the porthole at the night sky. It wasn't quite as black as it had been. The sun was pushing at the horizon and the stars were beginning to fade.

Gerber moved to the left and looked over the man's shoulder. There wasn't much to see, just a black expanse of ground broken by the silver of rice paddy water. He couldn't see the Song Ma, but was sure they had to be close.

"Get ready," warned the loadmaster. He was connected to the cockpit by a long black cord hooked into the intercom system. It allowed him to walk the length of the plane and still receive instructions from the pilots.

Gerber turned and faced Fetterman. He reached out and jerked on the harness and straps that wrapped Fetterman. When he finished, Fetterman did the same for him. Then each examined the other's back. That done, Fetterman moved up so that he would be the first to jump.

The loadmaster opened the troop door, pulled it in and then pushed it up out of the way. As he did, there was a sudden roar of wind, and the odors of North Vietnam filled the plane—warm, moist air that stank of too much fertilizer.

Gerber looked at the two tiny lights on the doorframe—one red, the other green.

Fetterman turned his head and shouted over his shoulder, "I hope Maxwell got these guys briefed right."

"One minute," shouted the loadmaster.

Fetterman centered himself in the doorway, a foot or so back. He peered out at the horizon, which was a black line almost at eye level. Above that was the sky: charcoal pricked by pinpoints of fading starlight.

"Thirty seconds."

Fetterman stepped up and put his hands on the doorframe, turning so that he could watch the glowing red light. Gerber was right behind Fetterman. He heard the loadmaster shout the time and tried to see if there were any recognizable landmarks. In the dark he'd have to rely on the talents of the pilots. He hoped the navigator knew his job.

Just before they jumped, Gerber noticed that the other men were on their feet, moving to get their equipment. He had hoped they were going to jump into Laos, or somewhere deep in North Vietnam. Now it looked as if the men were going out close to him.

Before Gerber could say anything, the loadmaster yelled, "Now!"

Fetterman was out the door the second the light flashed green, and Gerber jumped right behind him. Almost immediately the chute popped out and Gerber jerked sharply. He looked down at the silver ribbon of the river and hoped it was the right one. The ground was still black with nothing visible. In the distance the roar of the plane's engines faded. He twisted his head and saw the four faint plumes of flame from the jets of the turboprops.

Glancing left, he saw that Fetterman's chute was fully deployed. The master sergeant pulled at the risers, trying to keep himself over the water. A moment later, while he was still fifty feet in the air, Fetterman pulled the pin on the quick release, jettisoning the lower part of the harness. He turned toward Gerber, seemed to shrug, then dropped out of the chute and into the water with an impressive splash.

Gerber followed the same routine, falling free of the chute so that it wouldn't drag him down once he was in the water. As he surfaced, he jerked the cord on his life jacket and felt it inflate. Then, bobbing on the surface of the water, he searched for Fetterman.

When the two Special Forces men were reunited, they grabbed each other's harness. Then, face-to-face, they floated into the center of the river, moving with the swiftness of the current. Around them the jungle was beginning to awaken: birds whooped and monkeys screeched.

Fetterman leaned close to Gerber. ''Where'd those other guys jump?''

''Don't know.''

''Shit!''

''My feeling exactly.'' He glanced westward, but there was nothing to see except the curving riverbank and the blackness of the jungle. Overhead the sky was pale with only a few of the brightest stars still visible.

Gerber pointed toward the bank and Fetterman nodded. The master sergeant released his grip and the two of them began swimming toward shore. Once there, they moved along it carefully until they found a log about two feet long and nearly a foot in diameter. They guided it out toward the center of the river and held on to it, knowing it would provide cover.

As the sky brightened, Gerber began to study both riverbanks. He searched for one of the landmarks he had memorized before the mission, wanting a sign, something familiar, to show that they were on the right river and that they were close to the bridge at Thanh Hoa.

The terrain looked right. There were high hills to the south, all of them covered with heavy jungle, while near the water's edge light jungle reigned, with tree branches and bushes hanging in the water.

Neither man spoke as they drifted along. The water was luke warm and would have been comforting in the afternoon heat. Now it was clammy, seeping into their boots and under their equipment.

Finally, in the distance, Gerber saw a wide bend in the river. It swept around to the south, hiding the river from them. He reached out and tapped Fetterman's shoulder, pointing toward the bank. Fetterman nodded, and they began to drift in that direction.

When they reached shallow water, they stood and worked their way up the bank. Gerber hesitated, looking suspiciously at the shore, then climbed carefully up it, trying to leave no sign he had been there. Once on dry land, he moved ten or twelve feet into the jungle and crouched at the base of a giant teak tree. He took his map out of a plastic envelope and opened it. With his compass he oriented himself, based on the terrain around him, the river and what they had seen.

Leaning close to Fetterman, he said, "Those CIA pilots dropped us right on the money. That's a point for them."

"How far to the bridge?"

Gerber turned the map around and showed it to Fetterman. He pointed at the bend in the river and then at the bridge. "Less than a klick."

"We stay on this side of the river, go overland, we should come out on the bluffs overlooking the place."

"Should," agreed Gerber.

"We can stay off the hilltop and avoid the antiaircraft defenses. Get a good look at the target."

Gerber nodded and pulled back the camouflage cover on his watch. With the sun now just above the horizon, he could see fairly well. "We're early. We made better time down the river than I thought we would."

Fetterman didn't speak. He turned and looked into the jungle. Giant trees, their trunks wrapped in leafy vines, thrust themselves a hundred, two hundred feet into the air. Their branches were woven together, forming a loose canopy. Under them were the branches of shorter trees, and along the ground were ferns and bushes. They wouldn't have too much trouble moving through the undergrowth, he thought.

Fetterman pointed east and Gerber nodded. The master sergeant started off, walking slowly, carefully, making no sound. Gerber followed, five, six yards behind, keeping Fetterman in sight. As they worked their way through the jungle, they tried to avoid crushing small plants.

After the first burst of noise from the denizens of the jungle, silence settled over everything. It was almost like walking through a morgue. Fetterman kept the pace brisk, but the air was relatively cool and the terrain wasn't very steep. It was an easy walk, and within thirty minutes they could hear the sound of traffic on the road near the bridge.

Fetterman waved at Gerber, and the captain ducked into the jungle, taking cover. The master sergeant moved forward slowly, disappeared for a few moments and then returned. He crouched close to Gerber. "Bridge is below us."

"Can you see everything you have to?"

"Not from here. I'll have to get down closer so I can look under it. No big deal. There's plenty of cover and there doesn't seem to be anyone on guard."

Gerber nodded.

"Figure we can work our way back to the edge of the river and follow the bank. Looked to be clear from there."

"It's your baby."

"Then I suggest we rest here for ten minutes, drink a little water and head out."

"Got it." Gerber pulled out his canteen and opened it. The water had a plastic taste, but was cool and better than nothing. As he handed the canteen to Fetterman, something rattled to the west. Gerber turned, looked, then glanced at Fetterman. "Sounds like someone's firing."

Fetterman nodded and stood up. Then, crouching, he said, "Heavy firing. Must be twenty miles away."

Gerber nodded. "Damn it, you don't think those guys on the plane with us have stepped into it already, do you?"

"Christ, sir, what else?"

"Damn that Maxwell, anyway. I knew this would happen. Those guys didn't look like they'd be able to walk around the block. Now they've alerted the enemy that someone's on the ground."

"If they're all captured, maybe there won't be a major search."

"They won't know if they got them all. They'll put out a net. We're going to have to hurry if we don't want to get caught in it."

"If you're ready, then," said Fetterman.

"I'm right behind you."

Fetterman, with Gerber right behind him, started down the slope toward the river. Gerber hoped the net wouldn't be thrown out for an hour or so, but he doubted he'd have that kind of luck. "Damn it all to hell," he grumbled.

6

MACV HEADQUARTERS
SAIGON

Maxwell sat at his desk, one foot resting on top of a secret folder, and watched as Pat paced the office. The white-suited CIA man leaned over and picked up a Coke can, but there was nothing left in it as usual. As he set it down, he wished Pat would leave, but the older man, a high-ranking member of the CIA, had no intention of getting out soon.

Finally Pat turned. "What was the last transmission from our team?"

Maxwell shrugged. They had been over it several times. Both had been standing by in the radio room when the transmission had arrived, so that both had heard it. They'd had a secretary type up a complete transcript of the radio traffic, which wasn't more than a single page.

Dropping his foot onto the floor, Maxwell opened the secret folder. "Heavy contact. They've surrounded—"

"Shit! Transmission ended abruptly. Means their radio was shot to hell."

Maxwell nodded. Although he knew the operator could have been shot, which also would have ended the transmission, he knew it had been the radio. The carrier wave had disappeared, meaning the radio had gone off the air. Either the op-

erator had turned it off, which he wouldn't have done, or the
enemy had destroyed it. That was much more likely.

"You don't think they were compromised by that other
team, do you? What's their schedule?"

"I don't think Gerber or Fetterman compromised them.
We've heard nothing from them, but they weren't supposed
to check in before noon. Those Sneaky Pete types don't like
broadcasting all over the place. Feels it tends to compromise
them."

"Sure," said Pat sarcastically. "They don't check in and
they're free to do whatever they want. I've worked with them
before myself."

Maxwell didn't respond. He merely nodded.

"Tell you what," said Pat, "when they do check in, why not
have them try to establish contact with our team? Find out
what's going on with them. How many radios did they take?"

"Just two small URC-10s."

"Then they can give one to our people."

Maxwell turned so that he could face Pat. "I'm not sure
that's such a good idea. They've got a specific mission to do
that's not related to our mission. It just made good sense to put
them on the same airplane."

"I don't believe that was a request, Maxwell. I believe that
when your two Sneaky Petes check in, you'd better tell them
to locate our people. Understood?"

"Yes, sir."

"Now, I'm going back to the radio room and see if there's
anything new."

"Yes, sir."

Pat walked to the door, then stopped. He turned and faced
Maxwell, studying the man for a moment. "I get the impression you've been here too long. You've lost your objectivity
and forgotten that the men in the field are there for one purpose and that's to do what we deem necessary. If you've lost
sight of that, maybe it's time for you to find other work."

Maxwell wiped a hand over his face, then rubbed his palm
on the thigh of his trousers. There was a dark smudge there

where he had wiped his hand before. He looked up. "I understand the job, but I also know that Gerber and Fetterman are a good twenty miles from our team. Probably more now that each team has had the chance to move. Telling them to find our team isn't going to make it happen. It's not like looking for missing people in the city."

"I don't believe I asked for a rundown on the problems they might encounter. I believe I told you to order them to make the effort."

"I'll pass that along when they check in."

"Make sure they understand that it's an order and not a request," said Pat. "These military men seem to understand the concept of orders better than they do that of requests."

"Yes, sir."

The man opened the door and stepped through. As the door swung shut, Maxwell shook his head and sat staring at the cinder-block wall. He wanted to scream or shout or pound the top of his desk with his fist, but didn't. He sat there knowing he could pass the instructions on or not. When they were received, if he did send them, he knew Gerber would ignore them. That was the thing about both Gerber and Fetterman. They weren't stupid, so it made no difference about the tone of the instructions. Request or order, Gerber just wouldn't do it.

THE AEROFLOT PLANE was parked away from all the others at the airport in Sweden. It was at the end of the terminal building, where the tourists rarely walked, almost hidden behind the structure of the building so that no one could get a good look at it.

Carla Phillips led Travis and the camera crew down the concourse until they came to the Aeroflot area. Although she couldn't have explained what she had expected, she was surprised that the Aeroflot area was so conventional-looking. The only real difference was that the railing separating it from the rest of the concourse was a little more substantial than the railings at other airline gates. The carpeting and the wall coverings were red and the clerks wore red blazers, but that was about the only indication that Aeroflot was the Soviet airline.

As they approached, Tim stopped and broke out his camera. He filmed as Phillips moved toward the check-in counter. As soon as the big lights came on, one of the clerks was on the phone. A second later a large man came around the partition behind the desk. He ran toward them, one hand up, trying to cover the lens of the camera. He shouted at them in a mix of Russian and Swedish. Dressed in a gray-green uniform, he had sandy-colored hair and blanched skin.

Phillips stood her ground. "Keep rolling." She turned toward the man and thrust the microphone at him.

He stopped, his hand still raised, trying to block the camera. Looking at Phillips, he said, "No picture."

"You show him our papers, Dick," said Phillips. As Travis opened his briefcase and pawed through it, Phillips asked, "What don't you want filmed?"

"No picture," said the man.

Travis found his documents and advanced on the Russian. He waved them in front of him, as if they were banners. Then, speaking slowly and louder than normal, he said, "We have permission."

The Russian dropped his hand and examined the papers. He shook his head. "No picture here. Hanoi, picture. No picture here."

Travis looked at Phillips, who was standing to one side, the microphone clutched in her hand, forgotten. "This could screw up the whole deal."

For an instant Phillips stood still, then jerked a hand horizontally in front of her throat. "Cut it. It's not worth it here."

As the cameraman packed up his gear, Phillips and Travis walked up to the desk. Phillips placed her passport on the counter and showed her North Vietnam visa. Travis added the letters from North Vietnam and the various permissions to cross frontiers and to pass over the Soviet Union.

The petite blond clerk smiled, nodded and said in heavily accented English, "Yes, you come here. We know."

"We can board the plane?" asked Phillips.

Still smiling, the clerk said, "You must wait. Have seat and we come for you."

Phillips picked up her passport and jammed it into her purse. As she moved to the chairs, Travis right next to her, she said, "I don't understand why they were so uptight about us filming in front of their counter. Hell, shows the world they're not the monsters we've come to believe they are."

"Don't sweat it, Carla. Let's just remember that our purpose is to see conditions in Hanoi and not worry about Soviet public relations."

Sitting down, she noticed that the windows had all been painted red. No one could see in and steal valuable state secrets. She pointed to the windows. "Talk about paranoid."

"Again, who the hell cares?"

"Maybe we should interview that clerk. Make an interesting sidepiece."

"You have a Russian interpreter with you?" Travis grinned and added, "Forget it. We're just riding on their airplane to Hanoi. Let's not go looking for interesting sidebars when we don't need them."

"Right," said Phillips, though she was still thinking about the documentary she could produce and sell to the networks. Every little detail would help.

Before she could do a thing about it, the clerk came forward and said, "Is time to enter the aircraft. You must follow me and no pictures."

Travis leaned close to Phillips. "Her English stinks, but she makes herself very clear."

Phillips checked her watch. "We're going to hit Hanoi about two in the morning."

"That means we'll be taken to a hotel and allowed to rest for a while. Best thing for you once you've flown halfway around the world."

They stopped at the tunnel entrance leading to the airplane. The clerk stood centered in the doorway so that no one could pass her and it would be difficult to see around her. After several seconds, she started forward again.

They entered the plane near the cockpit. The door to the cockpit was closed. As they turned right, Phillips was amazed to see that it looked like the first-class section of the American plane she had flown on. The seats looked a little threadbare and there were some minor stains, but they were wide and looked comfortable.

Again she was surprised by the similarity between Russians and Americans. She had thought she was moving into an alien environment, but it closely resembled the one she had just come from. She didn't know if the Russians, realizing the power she controlled with her access to the American broadcast system, thought of her as a propaganda tool, or if this was the norm. She'd have to keep her eyes open.

She and Travis were directed to seats. Tim and Paul were given seats right behind them, and a burly Soviet man stored their equipment in a large closet near the front of the plane.

Once settled in, Phillips turned and glanced to the rear. Unlike American planes, which had a bulkhead and curtain to separate classes, this one had a solid wall and a door. She thought she could hear people in the rear of the plane, but with the quiet hum of the engines and the rush of air from the nozzle overhead, she couldn't be sure.

As Phillips turned around, the stewardess, a young, shapely woman in a tight-fitting jacket and short skirt, stopped in front of her. "You are our visitors from America?"

"Yes," said Travis.

"We make you comfortable. You want anything, you just have to ask for it."

"Thank you," said Travis.

As the stewardess retreated up the aisle, Phillips grinned broadly. "They're sure rolling out the red carpet."

"I think you'd better go easy on the smart remarks," said Travis.

"They're not going to do anything to add fuel to anti-Soviet sentiment in the States. Besides, if they handle us right, we'll give them good coverage. More valuable than money to them."

Travis shrugged. "Let's just not do anything to upset them."

"Of course not."

The airplane began to move then. Phillips leaned over to look out the window, but could only see a light rain falling. Runway lights glowed in the early-evening darkness. "We're on our way."

"Yeah," said Travis. "I just hope we're not going to be sorry about it."

"Why should we?"

"Who knows?" But inside he knew that flying into the enemy capital wasn't the smartest thing he'd ever done.

BY THE TIME Gerber and Fetterman reached the edge of the river, still hidden by the thick vegetation, the firing from the west had stopped. Not abruptly, but slowly, fading into random shots and then an ominous silence. Gerber's shirt was soaked with sweat, but not from the heat and humidity of the jungle. It was the tension of being in North Vietnam and knowing the enemy knew someone was around.

Fetterman crouched near the lacy branches of a huge fern that dripped water. The ground under it and him was soft. There was a slight odor of rotting vegetation and a stronger one of fish from the river.

He turned, looked at Gerber and pointed to the left. Gerber slipped in that direction, knelt near a rotting log and waited. From the east, where the bridge and the highway were, there wasn't much noise now, just the occasional rumble of a truck's engine, its tires on the surface of the bridge, and a single voice that shouted for thirty seconds and then stopped.

They stayed like that for a few minutes and then Fetterman stepped around the fern. He eased toward the bank of the stream but used the cover there to conceal himself. Satisfied there was no one at the water's edge, or waiting in ambush, he began moving downstream.

Gerber joined him, now in a slight crouch. He held his weapon in both hands, one hand near the trigger and his thumb on the safety. He kept his eyes moving, searching the jungle around him. He was aware of the growing heat and the high humidity. Sweat soaked his uniform and dripped down his face. Even with that, it was cooler than it would have been in the South. There was something about the jungles there. They seemed to capture the moisture and hold it in.

In front of him, Fetterman stopped and crouched. Gerber froze, waiting for Fetterman. The master sergeant waved him forward.

Gerber moved then, slowly working his way to where Fetterman waited. He stopped and turned, looking up. The bridge stood about a hundred yards away. He could see the concrete abutments, the underside of the spans, everything. Opposite them, on the other side of the bridge, sloping down toward the water, was a military installation—a semicircular arrangement of berm and bunkers that protected the antiaircraft guns.

Without moving any closer, Gerber knew what some of the guns were. Their shapes and barrels were distinctive. There were several ZSU-23s, each twin-barreled weapon requiring a crew of three to aim and fire it. Not far from them were the tracked ZSU-23/4s, radar-guided, four-barreled weapons.

Few soldiers moved around the camp. Most of them had probably gone somewhere else—maybe off to the mess hall for breakfast, or up to the bridge itself.

Fetterman, using a pair of binoculars, examined the structure of the bridge carefully. He whispered to Gerber, "Looks like the flyboys missed this morning."

"Doesn't matter."

Gerber took the binoculars and checked out the bridge himself. He could see that the abutments were thick structures sunk into the ground. Most likely they rested on bedrock and were heavily reinforced. All appearances, from the placement of the abutments to the way the spans crossed them, suggested a well-designed, sturdy bridge.

"No way we're going to destroy this," said Fetterman. "We'd need an engineering company and six hours to rig it right."

"And what, half a ton of explosives?"

"Minimum," said Fetterman. "Best we can hope for is to drop all the spans and do some damage to the abutments so that the repairs take some time. We can't eliminate it."

"You seen enough?"

"Shit, I've seen too much." He turned and worked his way close to the water. Stopping, he used the binoculars again. There was one major support in the center of the river, a thick pile situated so that a team might be able to get to it under cover of darkness. Fetterman was sure the center support could be rigged effectively. It was the bridge's only flaw.

Then, looking at the top, he could see searchlights just under the spans. The lights couldn't be detected from the air. They were designed to play on the surface of the water, making it that much harder for anyone to get close enough to destroy the bridge. The enemy wasn't taking any chances.

Fetterman dropped his binoculars and felt the enthusiasm drain from him. They had been given another impossible task designed by ground pounders in command who had never gotten into the field. It was a mission invented by managers who thought you just carried in a hundred pounds of plastique, tossed it at the bridge, then lit the fuse. They didn't know, or care to know, that blowing a bridge was a complex, technical job that required time and energy. To do it right was almost as hard as building the bridge in the first place.

He moved back toward Gerber and then froze. There was a crackling sound, as if someone was walking through the jungle not far from him. He knew it wasn't Gerber; the captain knew better. He glanced to the right and saw Gerber crouched on one knee, his weapon held in his left hand.

When their eyes met, Fetterman pointed at the sound and Gerber nodded. Slowly the captain slung his weapon and pulled his knife, holding it up so that Fetterman could see it.

Fetterman followed suit, then knelt and waited. There didn't seem to be more than one person coming. That meant it wasn't a patrol, just someone walking through the jungle, maybe a farmer heading to the river to fish. Through a gap in the vegetation, Fetterman glimpsed a khaki-colored uniform and an AK-47. The assault rifle certainly meant they weren't dealing with a farmer.

For a moment it looked good. Both Gerber and Fetterman were hidden in the shadows of the jungle. The soldier coming toward them had no reason to suspect they were there. With luck, the enemy would walk right on by. Once that happened, Gerber and Fetterman could slip away, retreat around the bend of the river and cross it. Then, on the south side, where it seemed there were fewer military people, they could cross under the bridge and return to the river.

But the enemy soldier stopped. There was no sound or movement. Fetterman could see a single shoulder covered in khaki cloth for a moment, then suddenly it was bare, as if the soldier had taken off his shirt. Bare skin glistened in the sun, revealing a slight shoulder and a thin upper arm.

A moment later the shoulder bent over, and Fetterman realized he was looking at a woman. She straightened, and he saw that she was now naked. Obviously she had slipped away to take a bath in the river. Fetterman couldn't believe the timing. Another few minutes and he would have been gone. At the moment the woman stood between him and the captain.

Then she started walking straight toward him. Her eyes were raised, as if she was watching something in the treetops. Slowly Fetterman raised his knife, getting ready to strike. And then he realized he couldn't kill the woman. If the enemy found the body, they'd know someone had been under the bridge. Now that the fake A-team had gotten caught by the enemy, killing the female soldier would compromise their mission completely.

The woman walked up to him and then stopped. Her eyes dropped and the color drained from her face. As she sucked in a lungful of air to scream, her eyes growing wide, Fetterman hit her once in the stomach. The air whooshed from her as she fell to the soft jungle floor and rolled onto her side. She wrapped her arms around her belly and squeezed her eyes shut as if she expected to die.

Fetterman stepped over her and unslung his weapon, pointing the barrel right at her forehead. She lay on her side, her knees hiked up as she tried to get her breath back. Slowly the wheezing stopped and she turned so that her eyes were staring up into Fetterman's. "You speak English?" he asked.

She didn't move or speak.

Fetterman reached down and jerked her to her feet. He could see she didn't have a weapon. That was obvious. Just then, Gerber appeared, carrying her clothes and weapon. He tossed the uniform to her and motioned that she should put it on. Fetterman glanced at the captain and shrugged. There had been nothing he could do about it. The woman had walked right up to him.

Gerber approached, and Fetterman whispered, "We kill her and we compromise the mission. We take her with us, they'll think she deserted."

"Then you propose we take her with us?"

"Nothing else we can do."

Gerber nodded. He knew the master sergeant was right. "Just one more thing to go wrong."

7

THANH HOA BRIDGE
NORTH VIETNAM

Fetterman stood in front of the woman and watched her dress. He noticed that, like the Americans who fought in the South, she didn't wear underwear. When she had slipped on her khaki shirt, black silk pants and Ho Chi Minh sandals, she picked up her pith helmet and put it on, shading her face.

Gerber used his knife to cut a strip of cloth from his own uniform. Using the narrow band, he bound her elbows behind her so that they were three or four inches apart. This gave her an unnaturally stiff posture—shoulders back, chest out— but it restricted the movement of her hands and nullified her as a threat, yet allowed her to move through the jungle with more ease than if her hands had been tied.

While Fetterman watched the prisoner, Gerber scouted the area, searching for signs that they had been there. He found some crushed grass, footprints and a few broken plants, but nothing that would give them away, nothing that showed Americans had been near the bridge.

Gerber then nodded to Fetterman. As the master sergeant turned, heading west again, Gerber moved up behind the woman. With his left hand, he reached out and touched her on the shoulder, pushing her forward after Fetterman.

As they walked through the jungle, no more than fifty or sixty feet from the riverbank, Gerber was aware of everything around him. There was an annoying, high-pitched wail issuing from the direction of the bridge. It sounded as if someone was using some kind of sandblasting equipment, or a concrete saw.

Twenty minutes later they rounded the bend in the river and the sounds from the bridge faded. Fetterman halted and crouched near the trunk of a palm tree. He took out his canteen and drank from it. Finished, he dribbled some water onto his go-to-hell rag and wiped the back of his neck.

When he finished, he offered his canteen to the woman. She stared at him for a moment, her eyes locked on his, and then nodded. Fetterman lifted the canteen to her lips and let her drink deeply.

Gerber drank from his own canteen and then put it back into its pouch. Kneeling, his eyes on the wide expanse of dark brown water, he remembered being told by a professor while at college that rivers should run clear and that pollution would soon darken the water. In North Vietnam river water was always brown, a mixture of silt and decayed jungle vegetation.

With one eye on the woman, who squatted on her heels in the classic Vietnamese position, Fetterman quietly said, "I'll cross first, check that side of the river, then you can bring the woman across."

"Water's not too deep here."

"That's going to be one problem," agreed Fetterman. "Probably have to crawl over the sandbar. At least the whole thing's underwater."

Gerber glanced upward at the leafy canopy that partially blocked the sun. Then he glanced at his watch. It was a little before nine in the morning—getting late in the day for a river crossing, but then he didn't want to stay put until nightfall. "Go," he said.

Fetterman nodded and made a quick check of his equipment, verifying that everything was fastened down. Then he glanced at their prisoner. She was watching his every move, waiting for a chance to escape. Shrugging, Fetterman moved down to the water's edge, using the vegetation as cover. The branches of the bushes dipped into the water, looking like people trailing their fingers in the river as they rowed. For a moment he hesitated, searching the bank opposite him, then looked back toward the bridge. It was hidden by the jungle as the river curved.

Satisfied there were no enemy soldiers around, no farmers who could see them, and no one coming toward the river to fish, he stepped out cautiously, avoiding the mud of the bank, not wanting to leave footprints or slide marks. Balancing himself with one hand on the dirt of the bank, he eased himself into the water, holding his rifle high.

The water closed over his boot and filled it. He had expected it to be cold and refreshing, but it was warm and slimy. Easing himself down into the water, he crouched and watched for signs of the enemy.

Slowly he moved out of the protection of the bushes on the bank, stepping tentatively into the sunlight as he studied the river. Now the water was above his knees and rising rapidly. As he continued, it reached his waist, soaking his uniform and equipment. Then he crouched and the water came up to his chest.

As he reached the center of the river, he glanced eastward, where the bridge was. He could hear traffic sounds on it—trucks, scooters and jeeps—and there was a babble of voices, as if all the guards were talking at the same time.

Fetterman kept moving. The water dropped away until it was about knee-deep. He crawled over the top of the sandbar, only his head and shoulders above water. Reaching deeper water, he floated away from the sandbar. A minute later he was lost in the darkness of the shade on the other side of the river.

He stopped in the shallows, the water flowing around his knees, and stared up into the blackness of the jungle. For a moment he couldn't see much because of the bright sunlight in the center of the river, but then his eyes adjusted. There were patterns of deep shadow and startling light—greens that were so bright they were nearly incandescent. From the flowers came a splatter of color—reds, oranges and yellows. And although there was the normal stink of mildew and decay, there was also a sickeningly sweet odor from the flowers, pushed by a light breeze.

Fetterman climbed from the water, being careful not to damage the vegetation or kick up a cloud of silt. The river was moving fast enough so that the silt would be carried away, but too much of it appearing might alert the men on the bridge.

Once he was out of the water, he checked the ground around him. There were no signs that anyone had been there recently. He moved off, ten or twelve yards into the jungle, then stopped. Crouching, he listened. Insects buzzed and monkeys chattered, not the obnoxious screaming that had marked sunrise, but a quieter, almost conversational level of noise. Glancing up into the trees, he saw a number of birds. They sat in the branches, looking hot and tired, as if it took too much energy to fly.

It was a jungle at rest, and that indicated there were no people around. Fetterman returned to the riverbank and stared across. He could see neither Gerber nor the girl, but knew they were there. The captain would have found a place to hide where he could also see across the river. Fetterman moved out into the water and waved a hand, his thumb up.

He retreated into the jungle and found himself a good hiding place. From it he could see the river. The girl was visible, moving through the water, which was already waist-deep on her. She moved carefully, walking slowly, afraid to fall. Gerber was behind, three or four feet back. He was close enough to strike her if necessary, or to grab her if she bolted.

At the sandbar she walked across as if she didn't have a care in the world. The water level fell until it was only knee-deep. Gerber, staying low, followed her as she moved into the deep channel. In almost no time she was in the shadows, Gerber right behind her.

They climbed up onto the bank, and Gerber pointed her eastward. She'd only taken a step or two when Fetterman appeared from his hiding place.

"Let's get going," said Gerber.

Fetterman turned and grinned at the girl. In rapid Vietnamese he told her that to cry out for help would mean her life. She might warn the men on the bridge that they were down there, but she'd die before any of the Vietnamese soldiers could help her. If she kept her mouth shut, they wouldn't harm her.

She stared at him, her brown eyes wide. She shook her head, and Fetterman asked her if there was something he'd said that she didn't understand.

In Vietnamese she said, "No. I understand. I'm surprised you can speak the language."

"You learn all that you can about your enemy. It's the way to fight a war."

"Sergeant," said Gerber.

"Yes, sir." Fetterman turned and moved off into the jungle. He wormed his way around and through the vegetation. He moved without touching anything, keeping his hands locked on his weapon. He moved slowly and silently.

Gerber and the girl followed a few feet back. The captain watched the woman, but she seemed resigned to her fate. She moved with the ease of someone used to the jungle. Her pace was steady and fluid. With her elbows bound behind her, she couldn't reach out and brush at the vines and ferns, nor could she swat at the insects that hovered around her face.

They kept at it for nearly an hour, walking slowly through the jungle, the sounds from the bridge becoming louder. Finally Fetterman halted and waved them to cover. Gerber pulled the woman back, and she knelt at the foot of a giant tree, its gnarled roots sticking up through the loose soil of the jungle floor. She leaned back, her head against the rough trunk. She was breathing through her mouth and she looked pale, as if the heat was beginning to get to her.

Fetterman worked his way forward until he could see the bridge again. Now on the south side of the river, looking back, he could see that his original assessment of the structure had been accurate. Someone had spent a great deal of time and effort building a bridge that wasn't going to collapse. He didn't know if it had been the French, the Japanese, the Russians, the Chinese or the Vietnamese who'd done it, and couldn't care less. What bothered him was the problem of destroying it.

On the south side of the river there were fewer enemy soldiers. The main antiaircraft batteries and SAM sites were on the northern side, where the ground was flatter, easier to work. On the south side a rocky cliff face jutted out, almost like a volcanic promontory into a lake. It was steep but covered with vegetation.

Fetterman returned to Gerber and leaned in close. "There's only a small contingent of men over here. They're all up on the road and the bridge. We stay close to the river, they won't see us."

Gerber looked at his watch again. "We've got a couple of hours to make the rendezvous."

"That shouldn't be a problem."

Neither man spoke for a moment. Fetterman took out his canteen, drank and then handed it to Gerber. When he finished, they gave some to the woman. As Fetterman put the canteen away, Gerber wiped the sweat from his face. His uniform hadn't dried after they crossed the river, and now he didn't expect it to, not until they got on the chopper heading out.

"Anytime you're ready, Master Sergeant."

"Yes, sir."

Again they moved off, heading south, away from the river, until they came to a rock wall. Fetterman skirted it, staying off the path that followed the wall. It was a well-worn path that showed the enemy patrolled the area regularly.

The path bent back toward the river, and Fetterman was forced to use it. If he avoided it, they would have to either float down the river, which would put them in view of the enemy on the bridge, or climb the rock face. Neither was an option.

He moved quickly until he was directly under the bridge. Once there, he stopped and looked up at the steel spans. Not much explosive would be needed to cut through them. That part wouldn't be a problem.

Having seen that, Fetterman continued on. Once clear, he moved from the path and waited. Gerber caught up to him, turned and looked back at the bridge. There were guards everywhere, and he could hear the rumbling of trucks.

Their observations completed, they started moving through the jungle, away from the target. The river took a shallow bend southward and the bridge disappeared. Fetterman didn't stop, though; he kept moving until they were more than a klick downriver. The channel had narrowed slightly, and deepened. The tallest and largest tree branches now met over it, forming a green canopy.

Again they stopped, and Fetterman asked, "Time to hit the water?"

Gerber took out his map and studied it. He made it three, four klicks to the sandbar and river bend where they would meet the chopper. The surrounding territory was empty—no cities, no villages, no known military installations. "Hit the water," said Gerber.

"We'll have to support the girl between us," Fetterman cautioned.

"And we'll have to watch her very carefully. I don't want anything to go wrong now."

Moving to the riverbank, they adjusted the life jackets and started into the water, pulling the girl between them. As the water got deeper, she began to panic, even as both Fetterman and Gerber grabbed and supported her.

In Vietnamese Fetterman said, "Relax. We're going to float for a while."

The river got deeper as the current carried them southeast. The water now seemed pleasant. Fetterman bowed his head and let it wash the sweat from his face. Suddenly he felt good, better than he should have, considering he was still in enemy territory.

They stayed in the shadows on the south side of the river. It took no effort to support the girl, and as the trip continued, her panic faded and she relaxed slightly. As they floated, Fetterman and Gerber listened for sounds of the enemy. No one seemed to be moving in the jungle around them. It was as if they were in virgin territory, an area devoid of people.

Floating down the river was better than walking through the jungle, Fetterman thought. Anything was better than trying to fight through the tangle of weeds, bushes, vines, ferns and trees. It was simple and quiet with only their heads and shoulders exposed.

After an hour they reached a place where the river widened. Rocks stuck up through the surface of the water, which was now only a couple of feet deep. They retreated to the riverbank and crouched in the shadows while Gerber checked the map. "No more than a hundred meters," he said.

Fetterman used his binoculars to study the bend in the river. There was nothing around that suggested the enemy was waiting. It looked deserted—an open sandbar, fifty feet wide and two hundred feet long. Bushes covered the side closest to the jungle, but none of them were more than two or three feet high. There was a hint of green, as if grass was beginning to grow on the sandbar. "Looks clear."

"Then let's get into position," said Gerber.

They slipped back into the water, swimming out toward the center of the river. The girl was supported between Fetterman and Gerber. They worked their way directly across the river, walking where it was shallow enough. Once across it, they halted again. Fetterman began to move toward the sandbar, staying close to the shore and using the bushes for cover.

Gerber watched the woman. She stood under the branches of a bush, watching as Fetterman crept toward the sandbar. The master sergeant disappeared and then reappeared, waving a hand. Gerber motioned the woman forward.

"Got us some good cover, Captain."

The master sergeant led them off the sandbar across a depression filled with stagnant, foul-smelling water. In the jungle there was a huge tree with a hollow in the trunk nearly four feet across. The two Special Forces men settled their prisoner in it and hunkered down on either side of her.

Once they were in position, Gerber took his URC-10 from its plastic protective pouch, extended the antenna and waited a moment. Then he heard the carrier wave and knew the radio was working. "Rescue, Rescue, this is Zulu."

There was a moment of silence, then, "Zulu, this is Cheyenne. Go."

"Roger, Cheyenne, we are ready for extraction."

"Roger, Zulu. Can you authenticate?"

"Standing by."

"What is your authentication number?"

"Four-six-two-one."

There was no immediate response. Finally the voice came back and said, "Roger, inbound to your location. Are you at the prearranged site?"

"Roger that. On-site and waiting."

"We are about one-five out."

"Roger," Gerber said. He reached up to collapse the antenna, then realized he had to keep the channel open. Now it was just a question of waiting for the helicopters and the support aircraft to get in.

And then came the second message. "Zulu, Zulu, this is White Twelve. Do you copy?"

Gerber glanced at Fetterman and rolled his eyes. Someone was on the air who had received his training in the Second World War. Gerber keyed the mike. "This is Zulu."

"Roger. Be advised that orders from Red River at MACV have been issued to you. You are advised that you must return to the DZ to initiate a search for a missing Alpha detachment."

Gerber wasn't sure what was being said. The operator, whoever he was, didn't know the proper call signs or procedure. "Say again," said Gerber.

"Roger. You are to initiate a search to determine the fate of the Alpha detachment that accompanied you into the November Victor area."

"Roger," said Gerber.

Fetterman moved in closer. "What the hell's that all about?"

"Christ," said Gerber, "it sounds like those assholes in Saigon want us to head back upstream to search for those men on the plane with us."

"Shit."

"Zulu, Zulu," the radio squawked, "this is Cheyenne. We are one-zero minutes out. Say hot or cold."

"Cheyenne, it is cold. I say again. It is cold."

"Roger."

Fetterman looked at the sandbar and the river beyond it. "What are we going to do?"

"Shit, Tony, those guys have to be twenty, thirty klicks from us. It'll take us a day, maybe two, to get back into position and begin a search."

"So we ignore the order?"

"What the hell else can we do? The CIA puts people into the field who aren't prepared to operate in the field. We can't be the ones who pull them out."

"Yes, sir."

"Besides, once we get back to our DZ, where do we start searching for them?"

"Zulu, Zulu, this is Cheyenne. Be advised we have been diverted from your mission."

Gerber squeezed the mike. "Negative. Negative. We are waiting now."

"Orders are to abort the mission."

"Christ," said Fetterman, "what the hell's all this?"

Gerber looked at the master sergeant. "I don't know, but I can guess that those assholes in Saigon are pulling strings to keep us on the ground so that we have no choice but search for their missing men."

"We going to search for them?"

"Shit, Tony, we're going to get the hell out of here." Gerber glanced to the rear and added under his breath, "I hope."

8

MACV-SOG
TAN SON NHUT
SAIGON

Major Jorgenson sat on the concrete floor in the rear of the SOG building and again counted the bundles that Sergeants Teppler and Tyme had pulled off the shelves. The small bundles held plastique, which many believed was the best thing to bring down bridges.

When he finished the second count, he stood, looked at the clipboard and totaled up the inventory. "Without detonators, det cord, primers and all the rest, I make it just over a thousand pounds."

"And that might not be enough," Tyme said.

"We'll need a team of ten men just to carry the explosives," said Jorgenson, "and we haven't even figured on weapons, food, ammo, water and everything else we'll need."

Tyme shrugged. "Well, sir, we might not need that much in the way of food, given the time frame once we're on the ground. Everything hinges on the explosives anyway."

"We've got to figure out a way to get the number of people down to something manageable. We can't go dropping ten, twelve people into the North."

Teppler moved from behind one of the shelves and set down another pack of equipment. "To do it right, we're going to need the E-tools."

"No way we're going to have time to fuck around with E-tools." Jorgenson shook his head. "I don't see a way to make this work. I don't even need to take a trip to the North to know we're not going to have enough time to rig the bridge."

"Well, sir," said Teppler, "we've still got to get ready for it."

"Certainly," said Jorgenson. He moved to the rear of the building and walked along the wall, looking at the racks that contained fatigues made in Germany and France and a bunch that had been stolen from the Soviets. Coming out from between the shelves, he tossed his clipboard onto the table and dropped into a wooden folding chair in front of the table. "This is a fucking waste of time."

"Sir," Teppler said, "we've got the other members of the team coming in for a preliminary briefing in case we decide we need to deploy within the next week."

"Doesn't matter," said Jorgenson. He was suddenly in a bad mood. He knew it was all a joke. There was no way a team could be sent in to blow up the bridge, not when it was surrounded by all the air defense the North Vietnamese could muster and was guarded by three or four hundred soldiers. The target was too close to Hanoi. Another five thousand soldiers could get to the bridge inside of an hour and it would take that long to rig the explosives properly.

He sat back and watched as Tyme and a clerk worked their way through a pile of equipment, sorting it out. Tyme was sweating, even though several huge floor fans blew air throughout the room. Their roar was almost more than Jorgenson could bear. "Listen, you guys, let's get out of here for a few minutes. I'll buy the beers."

Tyme turned. "I'm all for that."

"Yes, sir," seconded Teppler.

Jorgenson stood up. "There's really nothing we can do until we learn a little more. Without the specs, there's no way to know what we're going to need."

They started for the door. But it opened just as they reached it. Maxwell stood framed in the doorway. His hair was damp and plastered to his head, and the collar of his shirt was wet.

Jorgenson stared at the man. "Yes?"

Maxwell saw that Teppler and Tyme were right behind Jorgenson. He glanced at the men, then said, "I've got some bad news."

"Oh, shit," said Tyme.

Maxwell pointed. "Let's head inside where we can talk about it."

Jorgenson indicated the dayroom. "In there."

They entered the room and sat down. "What's happened?" Tyme asked.

"We've lost contact with the men in the North," Maxwell replied.

FOR A MOMENT Gerber couldn't believe his ears. There were men on the ground in the North, the pilots of the rescue helicopters and the covering fighters knew where they were and who they were, and now someone else was trying to recall the aircraft.

Gerber keyed the mike. "Cheyenne, Cheyenne, this is Zulu."

"Go, Zulu."

"Say status."

"Ah, roger. We have orders to return to base."

"Negative," said Gerber. "We need to get out now. We have information that is vital."

"Roger, Zulu. Wait one."

Fetterman leaned close. "What the fuck is going on?"

"I bet Maxwell or one of the CIA pukes has something to do with this. We've been set up on this from the word go. Now they've fucked up and they want us to pull their fat out of the fire."

"So what are we going to do?"

"We're going to get on the fucking chopper and get the fuck out of here. That's what we're going to do."

"Zulu, this is Cheyenne. Understand you are waiting for extraction."

"That's a roger."

"Inbound your location."

"Roger."

A moment later a lone aircraft flew over the bend in the river, a big prop plane that banked around, as if searching the ground for signs of the enemy. It climbed upward into the sky, disappearing behind a fluffy cloud.

"Zulu, do you have our aircraft in sight?"

Gerber keyed the mike. "Roger. A single A1-E Skyraider buzzed us."

"Do you have smoke?"

"Negative." The last thing Gerber wanted to do was pop a smoke to mark his location. That was the reason they had selected the bend in the river. It was a distinctive landmark and they wouldn't need smoke.

"Roger. Where are you?"

"East side, near the sandbar. We'll break cover as soon as we see the chopper."

"Roger."

Fetterman moved forward to the edge of the stagnant pool. He crouched in the reeds near a leafy bush, his weapon in his right hand. Turning, he faced east and searched the sky for the chopper. At the same time, Gerber reached into the hollow of the tree and pulled the woman out of it. He motioned her down and she knelt about twenty yards behind Fetterman.

From the east came the roar of piston engines. Two A1-Es flew over, turned so that they paralleled the river, then opened fire with their machine guns. Tracers streaked down and hit the trees. A few of them bounced back, tumbling. There was no return fire.

The planes then began a rapid climb, turning back toward the bend in the river. They began to circle overhead. As they did, the sound of their engines was overpowered by the heavy beat of helicopter rotors.

As soon as Fetterman saw the chopper, he ran out to the center of the sandbar and dropped to one knee. Gerber jerked the woman to her feet and pushed her forward. They crossed the stagnant water and stopped at the edge of the reeds and bushes, staying under cover.

The chopper turned toward them and began a rapid descent just above the treetops. It reached the edge of the jungle and flared, its nose lifting as it dropped to the sandbar. Fetterman bowed his head and shielded his eyes. The rotor wash tore at the sand, lifting it in sheets and spinning it around, creating a dust storm. The master sergeant faded from sight as the helicopter hovered, then slowly touched down.

As the chopper hit the sand, Fetterman was up and running. He scrambled into the hatch as Gerber jerked the woman up and propelled her forward. They hurried into the sandstorm, heads bowed. Through the blowing dust and whirling sand, Gerber could see the outline of the hatch. Fetterman was crouched in it, his hand extended.

Then, over the roar of turbines and the pop of rotors, came a burst of machine gun fire. Gerber barely heard it, but a single tracer flashed by him. As that happened, one of the A-1Es veered off and dived for the ground, its machine guns firing. Gerber slid to a halt near the hatch, grabbed the woman around the waist and tossed her up into the chopper. As he did, the enemy machine gun fired again, the rounds smashing into the thin skin of the fuselage. He saw holes appear next to him. Grabbing Fetterman's hand, the captain leaped upward and in.

A door gun began to fire then, its muzzle-flash stabbing out into the swirling cloud of dust and sand. Red tracers lanced out, hit the tree line and bounced away.

From overhead the Skyraiders attacked, using rockets, now that all the Americans had been identified. The jungle erupted in flashes of fire and smoke, and clouds of black dirt were thrown into the sky.

The helicopter lifted, hung in the air for an instant and then its nose dropped. They raced over the sandbar, leaving the dust and dirt behind them. Rather than climbing straight out, they followed the contour of the river, using the trees as cover. They flashed over the water, and then suddenly the nose lifted and they leaped skyward.

Gerber had to grab at the base of a troop seat, causing him to smash into a bulkhead, while the woman rolled back like a crate that had broken loose. Fetterman snagged her ankle and held on to her. The door gunner stood behind them all, hunched over his weapon, firing. The muzzle-flash was pale in the bright sunlight; the tracers looked pink and washed out.

Through the open hatch, Gerber saw the Skyraiders making their runs over the jungle. A fire burned, its black smoke rising like a gigantic exclamation point. And then they broke eastward, the Skyraiders racing after them. The door gunner stopped firing and leaned to the rear. The brass shell casings from his weapon rolled onto the floor under his feet.

Gerber looked at Fetterman and grinned. He held a thumb up. Fetterman nodded back and wiped a hand over his face. He rubbed it, smearing the camouflage paint and turning the carefully constructed lines into a nightmarish smear.

Through the hatch, Gerber saw the coast of North Vietnam flash by. They were suddenly over the South China Sea and safe from the enemy. It was a strange feeling. One moment in mortal danger, the enemy shooting at you, the next flying over the South China Sea, where the greatest danger was mechanical failure.

The woman sat up and stared at them. Now she looked frightened. Until the chopper had landed there had been a chance of escape or that the North Vietnamese would find them, but now that was no longer possible. She knew she was on her way to a POW camp, and that thought scared her.

Fetterman crawled around and untied her elbows. Once free, she moved away from him, shoving herself into a corner, away from everyone. Fetterman then looked at Gerber. Over the rumble of the engines and the pop of the rotors, he shouted, "Now what, Captain?"

Gerber grinned. "Now we relax for a few minutes."

TYME SAT IN THE DAYROOM, his face covered with sweat. It trickled down his sides and back. He felt hot, and it was hard to concentrate on anything being said. In front of him, Maxwell paced, picked up a magazine, then dropped it back onto the table. Finally the CIA man stopped moving and turned to face the men. He was pale and sweat dotted his forehead. He looked hot and miserable, too. "There isn't much I can tell you, either because I don't know or because it's classified—"

"Don't let that worry you," said Jorgenson. "We're all cleared here. You can tell us anything you want."

Maxwell pulled a handkerchief from his pocket and mopped his face with it. As he stuffed it back, he said, "There was a second mission. Gerber and Fetterman went in to look at the bridge. Another team was dropped about fifteen miles from them. It was a recon organized by us."

"Who made up this other team?" asked Tyme.

"That's something you don't have to know."

"Great!" snapped Tyme. "CIA."

"That's not what I said," countered Maxwell, but even as he spoke he knew everyone in the room knew. If it had been a Special Forces team, there would have been no reason to conceal the identity.

"What happened to the assholes?" Jorgenson asked.

"We're not sure," said Maxwell. "They walked into an ambush and we haven't been able to determine what happened after that."

"Has either the captain or Sergeant Fetterman checked in?" asked Tyme.

"Well, that's the one bit of good news," said Maxwell. "They came up on the Net just as they were supposed to. They requested exfiltration and the air assets were dispatched."

"But . . ." Jorgenson said, knowing from the tone of Maxwell's voice that there was more.

"Gerber and Fetterman were ordered to find out what happened to our missing team. They were supposed to go look for them."

"And?" Jorgenson asked.

"Last word was that the choppers were inbound to pick them up."

Jorgenson nodded. He knew what had to be going through Gerber's mind. They were in enemy territory without supplies for a lengthy stay. They were on a simple sneak-and-peek mission, then some bureaucrat in an air-conditioned office decided that since they were on the scene, they should go search for the missing men. There was absolutely no way for Gerber to succeed in such a mission. Gerber would get out and worry about explaining it to the bureaucrats when he returned. "What's that going to do to our mission?"

Maxwell looked around, then leaned back against the wall and wiped the sweat from his face. "I'm not sure. A reevaluation has been planned. Everything hinges on what Gerber learned in the North."

"I take it that means the Thanh Hoa bridge isn't a hot target anymore."

"No," said Maxwell. "It's still a priority target."

Tyme interrupted again. "Just what in hell was that other team doing in the North, other than compromising the captain?"

Maxwell took a deep breath and stared at the young sergeant. "That's something you don't have to know."

"Is our mission still on or not?" Jorgenson asked, refusing to let the CIA man drop the subject.

"You're on," snapped Maxwell. "I want you to get your gear together and get ready to move into isolation at the Bien Hoa complex."

"Why Bien Hoa?"

"It's separated from the press by nearly twenty miles. If it isn't happening in Saigon, a large number of reporters won't know it's happening."

"What's the time frame for the mission?" Teppler asked, speaking for the first time.

Again Maxwell mopped his face. He was uncomfortable talking to the soldiers, especially since it looked as if the CIA's clandestine mission into North Vietnam had compromised Gerber and the bridge raid. "We're looking to put you into the field in ten days, depending on what was learned in the North."

Jorgenson nodded. "Then we'd better get back to work."

"That mean you're not buying the beer, sir?" asked Tyme.

Jorgenson grinned. "It only means we're not going to drink it in the club. We're going to drink it once we get to Bien Hoa."

Tyme nodded and stood up. "Then we'd better get busy."

"Yes," said Maxwell, "you'd better get busy."

9

HANOI
NORTH VIETNAM

Unlike landing at an American airport where there was a sea of light, coming into Hanoi was like searching for an aircraft carrier hidden on a dark ocean. There were some lights, small glowing things that gave no hint that the North Vietnamese capital was near. Carla Phillips was sure the darkness was a result of blackout regulations designed to thwart American bombers. If there were no lights, there were no targets.

The plane touched down on the runway. Its engines roared and its brakes screamed, and Phillips was forced forward against her seat belt. As she rocked back, she glanced out the window, but could see nothing other than the dark shapes of the airport buildings and vehicles around them. When they reached the end of the runway and turned onto the taxiway, she was sure she glimpsed an antiaircraft battery. Dark, massive shapes with long, thin barrels stabbed the night sky.

The plane finally rolled to a stop near the terminal, and as they sat there, a stewardess moved to the front to open the door. The conditioned air evacuated with the speed of rapid decompression, and the humid heat of the tropics rolled in. There was a taste to it, a tangy, moist taste that was extremely unpleasant.

Within seconds, without having to move, Phillips found herself covered in sweat. It soaked her rapidly, making her uncomfortable as it trickled down her face and sides. When she wiped her face she was surprised at how damp she was.

"Christ, this is terrible," said Travis. "The humidity is going to destroy our equipment."

Phillips unfastened her seat belt, but before she could stand, a man entered the plane. He was small, with graying hair and a face that looked as if it had been chiseled from rough stone. His beard nearly reached his chest and he wore a khaki Mao jacket.

Standing there, near the cockpit, he surveyed the passengers until his eyes fell on Phillips. When he saw her, he moved toward her. "Welcome to the People's Republic of Vietnam."

Travis stood and held out a hand. "Thank you."

The man bowed slightly and pretended he didn't see the outstretched hand. "I am Vo Van Nguyen, deputy minister for International Press Relations."

"Richard Travis."

Phillips managed to get out of her seat and move closer so that she was standing just behind one of the seats. She bowed, holding her hands together as she had seen Yul Brynner do as the king of Siam. "Carla Phillips."

Nguyen bowed. "Welcome. We have transport waiting to escort you to your hotel."

"We have a great deal of equipment," said Travis, "and two of my people are in the back."

"Arrangements have been made," said Nguyen. "They'll be escorted to customs and checked in. If you'll come with me, we'll dispose of that unpleasantness quickly so that you can get to your hotel as soon as possible."

A hundred questions flashed through Phillips's mind, things she wanted to know and things she felt she had to know. She turned and glanced at the window. "It's very dark outside."

"Yes," agreed Nguyen. "We have to restrict the use of lights because of the bombing."

"I was under the impression," said Travis, "that Hanoi and the surrounding areas weren't among the approved targets."

"You'll find that what's reported by your President isn't always what's happening in Hanoi."

"That's what we're here to find out," said Phillips. She hesitated, then asked, "Is there much danger?"

Nguyen shook his head. "There's no more danger to you than there is to any civilian member of our population. Maybe less since you'll only be in Hanoi for a short time."

"Yes, well," said Travis.

"Please follow me," Nguyen said. He turned and walked slowly to the open door. A ramp led down to the darkened tarmac. Off to one side, near the nose of the jet, was a black car.

As they approached the car, its lights came on and its engine started. Nguyen opened the rear door and gestured, allowing Phillips and Travis to enter, while he himself got into the passenger seat. "I apologize for the lack of comfort, but we're a poor nation unable to afford the luxury of air-conditioning in our vehicles."

"No problem," said Travis. "I must say that your command of English is amazing."

"Yes, I studied at one of your American universities just after the war against the Japanese."

As they began to move, Travis turned and looked out the rear window. "We've got our camera and sound crew on the plane."

"Again," said Nguyen, "don't worry about them. Others will help them with their equipment and we'll all meet at the hotel in an hour or so."

They drove a short distance, stopping at the terminal entrance. Unlike those in the States, this one was nearly dark. There was no evidence of anyone around. The driver leaped from the car and opened the rear door so that Phillips could get out. She exited and stood on the ramp, looking out across the airfield. In the distance were the shapes of small airplanes parked well away from the buildings. She guessed they were MiG fighters and wished there was some way to get pictures.

Nguyen got out of the car and noticed that Phillips was looking at the fighters. "For our defense. Your American bombers attack us here, but our planes never leave our airspace. We must defend ourselves as best we can."

"Of course," agreed Phillips.

Nguyen led them into the building. Again Phillips expected air-conditioning but was disappointed. It was as hot and muggy inside as it was out. Along the hallway were ceiling fans that turned slowly. Only a few lights pierced the gloom in the windowless building.

At the end of the hall they entered a larger area that had open doors at one end and waist-high counters at the other. Near the counters there were a few lights, but at the other end there was only darkness. As they approached the counters, a man left a cubicle and positioned himself behind a counter. Before they reached him, another man appeared, pushing a small hand truck that contained Phillips's and Travis's luggage.

When they stopped, Nguyen said, "I trust this is yours."

"That looks like all of it," Travis said.

The customs man looked at the closed suitcases and passed over them. There was no reason to antagonize the Americans; they wouldn't be smuggling anything in.

The formality completed, they returned to the car, the man with the hand truck right behind them. At the car the luggage was loaded into the trunk. They climbed into the car and drove away from the airport, which was surrounded by a high fence. The guards at the small gate paid no attention to them.

Again Phillips was amazed at how dark it was. There were almost no streetlights, and very little light filtered through the windows of the houses and buildings. They passed an area of destruction, a block that had been knocked down, the piles of rubble visible in the light from the houses nearby. A couple of white flags were planted at the corners, one of which had a large red cross.

Nguyen turned in his seat and looked at Phillips. "That was a hospital destroyed by bombing last month. Nothing else was hit."

"A hospital!" exclaimed Travis. "And nothing else was hit?"

"It seems your bombers wanted to destroy it specifically."

"Our President has said that the only targets are those of a military nature," said Phillips.

"Maybe he considers a hospital a military target."

"How do we know it was a hospital?" asked Travis.

Phillips dug an elbow into his side and whispered, "Shut up."

They continued their winding trip, moving from one dark street to the next. Along some of the streets were canals that reeked of sewage and garbage. Light reflected off the surface of the dirty water. They passed another building that had been destroyed by bombs. This one was roped off, and it looked as if some attempt had been made to clean up the damage.

"A high school. A great number of our students were killed by the bombs that fell on it," Nguyen informed them.

"Yes," said Travis.

The tour continued. Phillips noticed that they passed the same points time and again. Each time they turned it was at the ruins of a building or block of buildings. Each time Nguyen labeled the ruins a hospital, a school, a medical facility for the old or a training ground for youngsters. From his descriptions, it seemed as if the Americans were ignoring manufacturing centers, military supply depots and army camps. Instead, they were waging a war of terror directed at the civilian population.

Finally they pulled up to a huge building in the center of Hanoi. It was six stories high and faced a wide canal. There were two guards at the door armed with AK-47s. One of them opened the rear door of the car so that Phillips could get out. She stood and looked into the canal next to the street. The water was dark and had debris floating in it. The odor was so heavy it seemed to hang in the air.

"Please," said Nguyen, gesturing at the door of the hotel.

They climbed the three steps that led into the hotel. A double door opened into a huge lobby. Phillips was surprised by the construction of the lobby. It was a cavernous area with tall marble pillars, a light marble floor and teak wainscoting. There was a large registration desk made of wood, with a long wall of pigeonholes behind it. Massive chandeliers made of cut glass hung from the ceiling, but no lights burned in them. Instead, small lamps sat on the desk and on a couple of end tables next to Victorian couches and wing chairs scattered throughout the lobby. Near one group of chairs was a massive fireplace. It was clean and polished, indicating that if it was ever used, the event was rare and the cleanup immediate.

"Wow!" said Phillips.

"Yes, it's a relic from the days of French colonial domination and oppression," Nguyen said sourly. "Our foreign guests seem to expect this sort of wasteful opulence."

Travis started for the desk, but Nguyen stopped him. "Everything has been taken care of. You'll retire to your rooms now." He took them toward a wide staircase hidden at the far end of the lobby. "I'm afraid the elevators aren't serviceable, but your rooms are only on the first floor. Not much of a walk."

At the top of the stairs they turned down a dimly lit hallway. Phillips noticed that the carpeting was worn and the walls dirty. It was nothing obvious, just the beginning of the decay that marked a hotel declining from four-star status to three-star.

They stopped in front of a louvered door painted white. The brass handle was slightly tarnished. Nguyen opened the door, leaned in to turn on the light, then stepped back. "Miss Phillips."

She moved into the room, which contained a large bed, a wardrobe, a wing chair and a table. At the foot of the bed there was a rack for her suitcase. Above the bed a ceiling fan tried vainly to circulate air, while a single lamp burned on the table. The window was covered by a thick curtain.

Nguyen followed her gaze. "When the light is on, the curtain must be closed. Part of our blackout regulations to thwart the Americans' aerial efforts."

"I understand."

Nguyen turned. "If you'll follow me, Mr. Travis."

"Right." He looked at Phillips. "I'll see you in a few minutes."

"Of course."

When the door closed, Phillips turned off the light and moved to the window. She jerked the curtain aside and threw open the sash, expecting a cool breeze, but the outside air was hotter and wetter than that in the room. At least the ceiling fan created some movement.

She unfastened the first two buttons of her blouse and blew between her breasts. Cool for a moment, she studied the scene in front of her, unsure of what she had expected. Certainly not a city like the one they had seen on the way to the hotel, or like the one she could see now. There were buildings, five, six, seven stories high, and there was some light, but nothing remotely resembling the neon display found in any American city. She could see the dark outlines of buildings, the roofs of some cluttered by antiaircraft artillery. It was a quiet, dark city that sweated heavily.

She turned away from the window and continued unbuttoning her blouse. As she shrugged out of it, letting it drop to the floor, she kicked off her shoes. She had worn too much clothing for the tropics.

Finished undressing, she stood naked in the dark room. Slowly she turned, taking in the impressions that washed over her like the humidity in the air. There was the heat and the quiet and the dark, but mostly there was the heat. If asked, she couldn't have told anyone what she had expected, but it wasn't a big, quiet, dark city.

As she moved toward the door on the right, which she assumed was the bathroom, there was a tap at the door. "Yeah?" she said.

"Travis."

"Wait a second. I'm not decent."

Travis rattled the knob. "I know that. Let me in."

She stepped into the bathroom and saw a small towel, an old tub that stood on claw feet, a sink with a rust stain in it and a toilet that looked as if it had been built by the inventor. Quickly she moved to her suitcase, lifted it to the rack and pulled out a robe. As she put it on, she wondered what had possessed her to bring such a garment. It was one of the many things she could have done without in the tropics.

She moved to the door and opened it. Travis stepped in quickly, like a fugitive avoiding the police. He glanced at the open window and walked over to it. Shutting it, he closed the curtain and told her to put on the light.

As she did, she asked, "What's going on now?"

Travis took his time looking at her in the dim light. Her robe was short and belted at the waist. Sweat dripped from her face and down her chest. "You look good," said Travis.

"We're here on business," she reminded him.

"That wasn't always your attitude," said Travis. He took a step toward her, and when she didn't retreat, he took another. When Phillips failed to move away, he reached up and put his hands on her shoulders, slipping his fingers under the fabric.

"Please," she said, but she didn't move and the word was spoken quietly.

Travis pushed the robe off her shoulders. It slid down her arms and then stopped, the belt holding it around her waist. He untied the belt and let the garment fall to the floor so that she stood naked in front of him.

Phillips looked up into his eyes but didn't move. She was filled with emotions and didn't know which one she wanted to win out. She wanted to turn her back, she wanted to put on her robe, she wanted to kiss him. Instead, she stood and waited.

Travis moved his hands down until his thumbs brushed her nipples. He rubbed them lightly, waiting for her to respond in some way. Finally she pulled away and stooped to pick up her robe. With her back to him, she put it on, belted it, then turned to face him.

"What's this?" he asked.

She shrugged. "Maybe it's just too hot."

"That's a new one. I'll give you that." He stepped to the chair and sat down. Wiping his arm across his forehead, he said, "You might be right about it, though. It is hot. I wonder how they can stand it."

"If you'd lived here all your life, you'd be used to it." As she spoke, she remembered something her mother had said to her while they had toured an auto assembly plant. Phillips, only eight, had asked how the men stood the constant, driving, pounding noise around them. Her mother had told her that the men got used to it. That comment covered a variety of sins. They got used to it.

"I suppose so," said Travis. He waved a hand in front of his face in an attempt to fan himself.

Phillips turned and looked at him. She realized he hadn't tried very hard to get her into bed. Once he wouldn't have taken such a halfhearted no for an answer. He would have pushed a little harder, trying to see if she meant it. He would have stopped if she had made it clear, but he wouldn't have quit so easily.

Travis took a deep breath. "What do you think of this so far?"

Now she was thoroughly confused. He hadn't come over to talk about the story, had even managed to get her out of her robe, but then had given up. Now, suddenly, he was talking about the story.

"So far..." she said. "So far it seems that our Air Force has missed all military targets." She shrugged. The last thing she wanted to think about was the story. She wanted Travis to take her into his arms and hold her.

As she looked at him, she tried to understand her emotions. Why was she suddenly so scared, depressed and vulnerable? Why did she want to make love to Travis but not tell him that? Why was she waiting for him to make the first move?

"Seems to me," he said, "that we don't know that. We've been shown some damage that they claim was the result of American bombing."

"What else could it have been?" she asked mechanically.

"Hell, I've seen blocks like that in the States. Urban renewal. Maybe it's the same thing here, but now they have the chance to make us look bad."

"Not us, the Administration."

"Whatever," said Travis wearily.

She turned, holding her robe closed. Travis was slumped in the chair, his eyes shut. His hair hung in his face, damp with sweat. He didn't look comfortable.

"Tomorrow?" she prompted.

"Tomorrow we'll play it by ear, see what they have to show us and hope someone slips up so that we can find out the real story."

Phillips moved to the bed and sat down. "You think they'll lie to us?"

"Oh, hell, yes, just as the Administration would lie if it was in their self-interest. Everyone lies about everything. You just have to be able to figure out the truth."

"Everyone lies," she said, thinking about some of the things he'd told her in the past.

Travis opened his eyes. "Everyone lies, but not all the time. That's the other trick. To know when they're lying and when they're not."

"I'll remember that," she said.

Travis stood up and stared at her. "Tomorrow's going to be an interesting day. I guess I'd better get back to my own room."

For an instant Phillips was going to stop him. She almost said something, and then the moment passed. It was too late. Besides, she didn't know how the North Vietnamese would respond to their sleeping together. To cover her sudden embarrassment, she asked, "Where's the crew?"

"On the floor above us. I asked Nguyen and he said they were being taken care of."

"I wonder what that means."

"Who knows? In some places that would mean there's cold beer in the room and in others a woman waiting. Anything to get a favorable story." He moved to the door, pausing, his hand on the knob. "Guess I'll see you in the morning."

"I guess so."

As he closed the door, she stood and almost ran to it. But then she thought about it and realized that to do so would put the relationship back into his hands. That wasn't something she wanted. Instead, she walked into the bathroom and filled the tub with water that never got very hot. She didn't care about the water temperature, though. All she wanted to do was wash the sweat from her body so that she could relax in bed.

She climbed into the tub and let the water climb to her chin. As she did, she realized just how tired she was. It would be good to get into bed without having to worry about pleasing someone else.

10

TAN SON NHUT
SAIGON

Gerber sat on the troop seat, leaning back into the webbing, and waited for the naval air transport plane to descend into Saigon. Only a moment before he had been standing in the rear of the aircraft, looking out at the brightness of Saigon. The whole center of the city seemed ablaze with light. All Gerber could think of was how easy that made it for enemy gunners. They didn't need aiming stakes or spotters. They just aimed into the center of the light, knowing they would hit something.

As they had neared the city, Gerber had returned to his seat and buckled in for the landing. Fetterman sat next to him and the woman they'd captured was next to Fetterman. At first the commander on the aircraft carrier had been reluctant to let her out of the brig to fly on one of his transports, but Gerber had convinced him. Now, as they approached Saigon, Gerber wasn't sure it had been such a good idea.

On the ship they'd only had time to take a shower and change into fatigues supplied by the Marines. That finished, they had collected the woman and headed up to the flight deck where the transport waited. Normally the plane would have stopped at Da Nang to let Gerber and Fetterman find another way to Saigon, but the crew had wanted a little shore leave in Saigon and the CO had approved it.

Now Gerber sat there, strapped into his seat, and let the pilots and crew do their job. After so many rides in the cargo areas of so many aircraft, Gerber no longer worried about crashing. The men who flew the planes and helicopters were as good at their jobs as he was at his. They might not make the best infantrymen when put on the ground, but in the air they couldn't be beat. The military had become highly specialized. Everyone had a job to do, but no one was good at anyone else's job.

There had been a time when everyone in the Army was an infantryman first. Once they had mastered that skill, they learned other jobs, but in the end they were infantrymen. Now the Army granted eight weeks of training in the art of infantry warfare and then the men moved on to AIT. In some cases that meant another eight weeks of infantry training, but all too often it was Advanced Individual Training. Clerks went to clerk school, cooks went to cook school and pilots went to flight school. At least when they got out they knew their jobs.

Even if he had been worried about the skill of the pilots, he didn't have time to get scared. Before he realized it he heard the whine of the servos, announcing the lowering of the landing gear. He turned, but the window was too far away for him to see anything.

And then they were on the ground. There was a roar as the engines were reversed, and they were thrown forward as the brakes were applied. A civilian pilot with such a heavy foot would have lost his job for scaring the passengers, but a military pilot was handed a medal instead.

They taxied back toward the terminal, and as they rolled to a stop, Gerber unfastened his seat belt. He got up and turned so that he could keep an eye on the woman they'd captured. He was aware of the hatch being opened and a flash of white.

Maxwell moved among the other passengers and stopped next to Gerber. ''Man, are you in trouble.''

"Hi, Jerry," said Gerber. "Nice to see you again. How are things?"

Maxwell looked around wildly and saw that there were too many other people on the plane. "We have to talk."

Fetterman unfastened the seat belt of the woman and helped her to her feet. Maxwell watched all that and snapped, "We don't have time to mess with women."

"Now, Jerry," said Fetterman, "you let us worry about all that. There are important things going on."

Maxwell looked to Gerber for help. "We've got to talk and I have to get you two up to Bien Hoa. There are some very angry people at MACV."

"What the hell's going on?" Gerber growled.

Again Maxwell looked around. Lowering his voice, he said, "There have been some real problems in the North."

"Shit, Jerry," said Gerber, "everything went off for us. There wasn't much else we could do."

The plane was nearly empty. Maxwell started toward the hatch. Gerber claimed his weapon and equipment and followed. Fetterman did the same and let the woman lead. They climbed down to the tarmac and stood in the hot wind blowing from the east.

"I've got a jeep waiting," said Maxwell. He walked off toward it.

Fetterman joined Gerber, who was watching Maxwell move away. "What the hell's his problem, sir?"

"I think he's miffed that we're back without learning the fate of his fake A-team. Now he's trying to get us up to Bien Hoa in a hurry."

Fetterman shot a glance at their prisoner, who stood there with them, her eyes wide as she tried to take in everything she saw. "So what's happening?"

"Damned if I know," said Gerber.

Maxwell had reached his jeep and turned to find that neither Gerber nor Fetterman had followed him. He stood there, one hand on his hip, gesturing for them to join him.

"Think we should?" asked Fetterman.

"Hell, he'll have a heart attack if we don't. Seems to be quite important to him."

They started for the jeep, and as they did, Maxwell hurried toward them. "Not the woman," he said again. "I told you to forget about her."

"Jerry," said Fetterman in a tone reserved for a child who wouldn't listen, "if I took orders from you, it would be different, but I don't. You can suggest things and then I can either act on them or not as the mood moves me."

"Very well," said Maxwell, "I suggest you arrange to meet the lady later. We have business now."

Fetterman laughed. "But you don't understand. She's our prisoner."

"What . . . ? No one said anything about a prisoner. Where in hell did you capture her? We've got to get rid of her."

"We're not turning her over to MI," said Gerber. "They won't get anything from her, and they'll have to turn her over to the South Vietnamese."

"She can't go with us," said Maxwell.

"Fine," said Fetterman. "We'll find our own way up to Nha Trang and turn her over to the Fifth Special Forces there. That way something good will come of it. We won't be creating a hard-core enemy."

"You can't do that," said Maxwell.

Gerber shifted his weapon to his left hand and put his arm on Maxwell's shoulder. He spoke to him softly so that no one else could hear. "Jerry, you haven't gotten the big picture yet. Your boys sent us on a jerk-off mission that didn't mean shit as a cover for your other mission, which went right into the toilet. Now, I don't work for you. We're going to take care of our prisoner."

"But—"

"There are no buts, Jerry. I'm telling you how it is in the real world."

Maxwell shrugged the arm from his shoulder and turned. He glared at Gerber. "The real world? You want to hear about the real world?" He had screamed the last few words. He looked around, making sure there was no one to listen, and lowered his voice. "In the real world, you're in the shit locker. Your orders were to learn the fate of the other team and you chose to ignore those orders. I've one man trying to see Westmoreland or Abrams and have your ass for breakfast. I come down here to meet your plane and get you up to Bien Hoa before the shit can begin to rain down on you, and all I get is stories about the real world."

"Okay, Jerry," said Gerber, getting angry. "This is getting us nowhere."

Maxwell took out his handkerchief and mopped his face. "What are you going to do with the woman? You can't take her to Nha Trang. There isn't time."

"Well, Sergeant Fetterman and I will stroll on over to SOG and see who's around. We'll turn her over to one of those guys to take up there."

"All right," said Maxwell, stuffing his hankerchief into his pocket. "But we have to hurry."

"Tony," said Gerber, "let's go."

They all walked toward the jeep. Fetterman got into the rear and held out a hand for the woman to take. Gerber got into the passenger side and Maxwell climbed behind the wheel. Before he started the engine, he repeated, "We have to hurry."

He drove across the ramps, dodging around the revetments of parked fighters, and pulled up in front of the SOG building. Gerber hopped out, watched as the woman got out, then let Fetterman take her into the SOG building.

As Fetterman went inside, Gerber turned to Maxwell and asked, "You didn't actually expect us to go find your missing people, did you?"

Maxwell stared straight ahead and shrugged. "I didn't think you would."

"Couldn't," said Gerber. "We didn't have the supplies to do it and we didn't know where they were, what they were doing, or have any codes and authentications to prove we were good guys. They might have shot the shit out of us before we could have gotten close."

"You could have made an effort."

"Jerry, we were twenty, thirty miles from them. The first time we saw them was on that plane. The fact they went in so close to us could have compromised *our* mission, but no one seems too concerned about that."

"You job is to do as you're told."

"Not by you, Maxwell," Gerber shot back. "Never by you or your suit-and-tie friends."

There was silence for a moment. Maxwell coughed. "They didn't last very long."

"Christ, Jerry, what did you expect?" Gerber turned to look at the CIA man. "They didn't know what they were doing. We could tell that from the way they wore their uniforms. Hell, it was obvious they weren't Special Forces."

"How could you tell?"

"For one thing, they didn't know how to wear the beret. For another, they all had on brand-new boots. Brand-new uniforms is no big deal, but no one who knows anything would jump into a jungle wearing new boots. Just what in hell were they supposed to be doing?"

"Their mission was classified. Only those with a need to know were consulted."

"Well, next time you superspooks decide to throw people into the jungle, you'd better talk to someone who's been there before."

"Yeah," said Maxwell.

Fetterman came out the door. He stopped near Gerber. "Found a sergeant to escort her up to Nha Trang. That should take care of the problem for now."

"Good. Once we're clear, we'll take a ride up there and see how she's doing."

Fetterman climbed into the rear of the jeep. "You find out why Jerry's so hot to get us up to Bien Hoa?"

"Not yet," said Gerber, "though I think I have a pretty good idea."

Maxwell looked over his shoulder. "There are a few people running around here who think you should have made more of an effort to find our missing men...."

"Well, hell, Jerry," Fetterman began.

"I already filled him in," said Gerber.

"Anyway," said Maxwell, "I've got a team in isolation up in Bien Hoa and I'm taking you there. You'll have everything you need to get ready for the mission to the Thanh Hoa bridge."

"Yeah," said Gerber. "That's something else we should talk about."

Maxwell drove them back across the airfield and over to Hotel Three. He stopped short of the fence and shut off the engine. Then, before anyone moved, he reached down for the chain bolted to the floor, looped it through the steering wheel and used a padlock to secure it.

"A chopper will take you to Bien Hoa and there'll be a jeep at the field there to take you over to the isolation compound."

"I have to tell you that I don't like this, Jerry," said Gerber.

"That's not my concern," said Maxwell. "I'm trying to do you a favor, and I'm more than a little sick of your attitude."

"Well, Jerry," said Fetterman, "if you'd leveled with us in the beginning, before we got on the plane, things might have gone a little differently. It's too bad everyone is so security conscious that they always step on their dicks."

"Everything you need is in Bien Hoa," said Maxwell, ignoring the comment, "and I played hell getting the chopper laid on."

Gerber climbed out. "Well, thanks for everything, Maxwell."

Fetterman followed him into the terminal. It was at the foot of the tower and looked as if it had been built as an afterthought. It had a dirty plywood floor, and behind the counter was a scheduling board. A bored Spec 5 sat behind the counter, reading a paperback novel. Opposite him were some chairs and sofas that looked as if they had been rejected by the Salvation Army. Several soldiers sat or slept on them.

Gerber walked up to the counter. "I'm scheduled for a flight to Bien Hoa."

The clerk marked his place in the book and set it down. He reached for a black three-ring binder and flipped a couple of pages. "You Gerber?"

"Captain Gerber, yes."

"Chopper's out there, Pad One, waiting."

"Thanks."

He turned and headed toward the door, Fetterman right behind him. There was only one helicopter with the engine running. Gerber ran toward it, a hand on his beret, holding it down. He ducked under the blades, jumped into the cargo compartment and sat on the troop seat.

The crew chief, dressed in a Nomex flight suit and wearing a flight helmet, leaned around and shouted, "You Gerber?"

"And Fetterman," said Gerber, nodding.

"Right, sir. Please buckle in and we'll get you over to Bien Hoa."

Gerber buckled his seat belt as Fetterman climbed on board. The master sergeant stepped around the captain and sat down with his back to the transmission. Almost as he sat down, the sound of the turbine changed. It began to roar, and the aircraft was suddenly light on the skids.

A moment later they took off, climbed up past the tower, turned east and headed into the brightness of the night lights of Saigon. Gerber watched it all out of the cargo compartment door as the wind rushed around him, threatening to steal his beret.

As he watched the sights below him, people moving through the artificial daylight of neon and electricity, he shifted and looked down at the black ribbon that wormed out of Saigon—the Song Sai Gon, the river that gave the city its name. He had taken this trip a hundred times, and each time he found a new reason to be amazed about it. Maybe it was the optimism that showed. The South Vietnamese were building and playing as if the war and their world would last forever. Gerber knew it wouldn't, couldn't be like that. Already there were those in power in Washington who were talking about getting the Americans out of Vietnam.

He turned his attention from the ground and looked at the instrument panel, which was visible between the pilots' seats. A light red glow barely lit the panel. Gerber couldn't see the instruments, but assumed the pilots could. They were the ones who had to look at them.

A few minutes later they made their approach into Bien Hoa. They didn't land at the airfield, though. Instead, they were headed for a pad situated on the southeastern side of the camp. The landing lights illuminated it. Gerber could see a jeep and driver on the ground.

They began to hover, and the jeep disappeared in a cloud of swirling, blowing dust. The jeep's driver bowed his head and held on his beret with his right hand. They touched down and the crew chief tapped Gerber on the shoulder. "That should be your ride, sir."

Gerber unbuckled his seat belt and dropped to the pad. He hurried off as Fetterman joined him. Once they were clear, the chopper took off, and in seconds all was quiet. Gerber glanced into the jeep. "Good evening, Justin."

"Evening, Captain. Glad you could make it."

Fetterman scrambled into the back, put his feet up on one side of the jeep and leaned his head back against the radio mounted on the other. "Home, James," he said.

"Evening, Tony," said Tyme.

"Good evening, Justin."

As Tyme put the jeep into reverse and backed away from the pad, Gerber asked, "What the hell's going on?"

"Major Jorgenson, Sergeant Teppler and a couple of new guys are in isolation with me for the mission to the North, now that you've completed the recon."

"Anyone discussing this thing seriously?"

Tyme shifted into first, and they lurched forward. Once he had them moving, he said, "We've got everything we need at the hootch, including the explosives."

"Yes," said Gerber, "I understand that, but has anyone thought this mission all the way through?"

"I believe Major Jorgenson has some thoughts along those lines."

They slowed down and stopped at a gate next to a one-man guard hut. The MP, dressed in jungle fatigues, came out holding a clipboard. He glanced at Tyme and nodded. "These the men you were to pick up?"

"That's right."

The MP flipped over a page on the clipboard. "Which one is Captain Gerber?"

"I am."

"Please give me your service number."

Gerber grinned and recited the number quickly.

"Thank you, sir." He looked at Fetterman. "Are you Master Sergeant Fetterman?"

"The same."

The MP went through the service number ritual again, then made a mark on his clipboard. When he finished, he said, "Thank you," and waved them through.

They drove to a hootch that was surrounded by another barbed wire fence. Tyme parked in front of it and they got out. Gerber recognized the place. They had staged out of here before. A long, low hootch with a tin roof and plywood walls and floors, it was filled with supplies taken from a variety of sources. There was an open bay used as sleeping quarters and a dayroom that had held almost nothing of interest the last time Gerber had been there. Everything they would need would be supplied. Hot food came from an Army mess hall and was brought in by truck. There would be a liaison officer who would take care of arranging food, beer and anything else they wanted. He would be their only outside contact.

Gerber moved along the walk made of two-by-twelves. Two had been turned on their sides and crosspieces had been nailed

to them, lifting the walk off the damp ground. As he reached
the screen door, he heard voices and saw a lamp on a table.

Jorgenson apparently saw him at the same time and stood
up. He waved at Gerber. "Come on in."

Gerber entered and stopped, looking at the equipment piled
in the center of the floor. It wasn't all standard Army issue.
Much of it had been manufactured in Europe and was to be
used on sterile missions into the North. The American government didn't want anything dropped in North Vietnam that
could be traced to the U.S.

"You look like hell," said Jorgenson.

"Must be these damned Marine fatigues," said Gerber.

"Well, I can take care of that problem, but we have others
that I'm not sure we can fix."

Gerber dropped into one of the chairs. After everything that
had happened in the past twenty-four hours, he was beat. Now
that he was back to where he was supposed to be, all his energy drained out of him. He rubbed a hand over his face.
"What problems are those?"

"How we get a ton of explosives to the bridge and have the
six to eight hours needed to rig it properly before the entire
North Vietnamese army arrives to shoot our collective asses
full of collective holes."

Gerber nodded. "Oh, those problems."

11

HANOI
NORTH VIETNAM

There was a tapping at her door that wasn't loud enough to fully wake her. It became louder, and Carla Phillips awoke, hot, confused and, for a moment, afraid. Then the realization of where she was washed over her and she lay back, staring up at the ceiling and the slowly spinning fan.

The knock came again and then a voice asked, "Miss Phillips, are you awake?"

"Yes, I'm awake."

"We have a number of tours scheduled for today, and breakfast is arranged, if you'd care to join us in twenty minutes in the lobby."

"That will be fine."

"Thank you."

She threw the sheet off, wondering what time it was. There didn't seem to be any sunlight, and she glanced over at the window where the thick curtain was pulled closed. She got up, walked over and opened the curtain, gasping at the brightness. The sun beat down into her room.

When her eyes had adjusted to the glare, she looked out on the city, which was modern, but with only a few cars and trucks. Off in the distance was a pile of rubble that looked like the remains of a bombed-out building.

The city streets were paved with brick, and she could see a canal, twelve, fifteen feet wide, with brown water in it. Two cars were parked downstairs, both of them black with flags on their hoods. She didn't recognize the make, but thought they were French.

Bicycles and pedicabs were the rule rather than cars and, along with the pedestrians, they filled the streets. Off to one side, away from the canal, on the wide sidewalk, was a long row of holes two to three feet in diameter. She'd never seen anything like them and had no idea what use they had.

Finally she opened the window. There was a slight breeze that smelled of ocean and sewer. Salt and fish and human waste. It wasn't a refreshing, cooling breeze, but a hot, wet one. Along with the breeze, the noise of the city swelled around her—voices and the buzz of small engines. A loudspeaker yelled at the people, but Phillips couldn't understand the words.

She turned and moved to the bathroom, where she spent a few minutes. Returning to the bedroom, she put on clothes that she felt projected the right image—a light-colored blouse, dark pants and boots, and a blazer. Then she walked back into the bathroom, studied herself in the mirror and decided she had the effect she wanted.

When she left the room, she noticed that she hadn't been given a key. But that didn't matter, since there was no way to lock the door.

Downstairs she stood in the lobby for a moment until Nguyen came up to her, smiling broadly. "Come, we've assembled in the meeting room."

Phillips followed him across the lobby and down a long, dim hallway into another room. As they entered, Nguyen closed the door, and she realized that the room was air-conditioned. A long conference table in the middle of the floor had been set up for dining. In front of each of the six chairs was a linen place mat, a variety of silverware, a china coffee cup, a water glass with a slice of lime floating in it, a juice glass, a bread plate and a dinner plate. A white napkin folded in a complex manner stood in the center of the dinner plate.

Phillips moved to one of the empty chairs. She nodded at Travis, who was sitting at the table, then at Young and Angstadt, who were sitting opposite him and looking uncomfortable. As she sat down, Nguyen clapped his hands, and the serving began. First a waiter in a waist-length jacket entered and poured orange juice into the juice glass. Next a woman, dressed in the traditional *ao dai*, served rolls, while another woman, dressed similarly, served eggs. At the same time a waiter brought in bacon.

Nguyen noticed that Phillips was staring at the food, but not eating any of it. "Is there something wrong with your breakfast?"

"Oh, no," she said. "It looks and smells delicious. It was just that I had hoped for something a little more, ah, traditional."

"I see," said Nguyen. "Well, I'm afraid our traditional breakfast isn't something the Western taste is ready for."

"Mr. Nguyen," said Phillips, "I came here to cover a story about the North Vietnamese fighting Americans. I fully expected to eat some things that weren't a normal part of my diet. I expected it because I need to see exactly how the people live on a day-to-day basis. I venture to say that this is a little more food than the average citizen sees for his breakfast."

"Then tomorrow we'll arrange something like that."

"Thank you."

Nguyen took a bite and then picked up a folder. He opened it and extracted a paper. "Today we're scheduled to tour the People's Hospital, which was damaged by American bombs. Just outside the city is the wreckage of an American airplane. You'll be allowed to photograph it and interview the inhabitants in the vicinity." He grinned. "You have an interpreter with you?"

"No," said Travis.

"That's no problem. We'll have someone available to fill the role, or if there are no objections, I'll handle the duties myself."

"You'll do just fine," said Phillips.

"This afternoon we'll tour a factory where medical supplies are packaged and we'll visit a hamlet, a farming community outside Hanoi. A number of the people there have been killed and injured by bombings."

"Is it strictly a farming community?" asked Phillips.

"Certainly."

"Then it shouldn't have been bombed."

"No," said Nguyen, "except that to kill our farmers is to end our support of our brethren in the South. Cut the food supply and you end the resistance to aggression."

"We'll certainly want to see that," said Phillips.

"The itinerary is all arranged."

Phillips attacked her breakfast, knowing that her place on the networks was virtually assured. Good footage of the bombed hospitals and the defenseless villages would get her network airtime, and that would prepare the ground for the really big story. She'd been in Vietnam less than a day and already she knew everything was going the way she'd dreamed.

IT WAS NOW MORNING. Gerber had eaten a big breakfast and was sitting at a table in the isolation area. The breakfast wasn't on par with those he'd ordered when in Saigon, but the eggs had been fresh and the juice cold, if not very tasty. Now, with the maps spread out in front of him, along with the notes Fetterman had made after the recon of the bridge, he could see the whole picture clearly. He tossed his pencil down and watched it bounce and roll off the table. "There really is no way."

Jorgenson, who was clad only in his OD Army-issue underwear, nodded. "You seem to have gotten the whole picture."

Fetterman, dressed in new jungle fatigues taken from the supply stores, said nothing. Tyme, wearing only fatigue pants and unlaced boots, said, "I think we can get in there. Hell, we can air-drop the explosives and float them down the river. We don't have to carry them."

Gerber spun one of the aerial photographs around so that it faced Tyme. He tapped it with his finger. "Getting the explosives in isn't the problem. It's getting the time to rig the bridge properly. We'll never be able to spend the five or six hours in there to do it."

Tyme scratched the back of his head and studied the pictures. He said nothing more.

"I think we need to get in touch with Maxwell and MACV and let them know the situation," said Jorgenson. "Tell them that it can't be done under the current circumstances."

Gerber leaned back, his fingers laced behind his head. "They're going to tell us to come up with a way to make it work. Tony, any ideas?"

Fetterman pulled a picture toward him and picked it up. "This is going to be a tough one."

Gerber nodded. "That's why we get paid the big money. We have to knock the bridge down. There must be a way to do it."

Teppler entered the room and dropped into the vacant chair. He looked at the map, the drawings made of the bridge and then a few of the pictures. "Time is the key," he said.

"Exactly," said Gerber.

"We can't get the time to rig the bridge properly."

Gerber stood and stretched. He walked to the door and looked out at the isolation compound. Red dirt stretched out to the fence about thirty yards away. Palm trees and bushes had been planted along it to conceal the compound from Bien Hoa.

He turned and walked back to the table. "A full-blown assault would work. A company of rangers to hold off the enemy while the engineers worked at high speed to rig everything. Take a battalion to do it right, and no one's going to give us that battalion."

"Nope," agreed Jorgenson. "The guys at MACV were raised on afternoon movies where two guys sneak in, stick some plastique to the pilings and the whole thing goes up.

They're going to wonder why we can't do that. We're supposed to come up with the perfect covert mission."

"Tony, you see any way to make this work? It doesn't even have to be a good plan, just one that has a chance."

"Captain, there's no sense wasting our time and possibly our lives on this one. The results would be less than spectacular. Seems to me the best course of action would be to have the Air Force boys keep dropping the spans each time they get them back up. A ground operation just isn't smart."

Gerber looked at the other officer. "Major?"

"I've studied this for three weeks. I've seen every picture ever taken and seen the bomb damage assessments. There's no way a small team can place enough explosives to take down the bridge. The enemy has too many troops guarding it."

"I believe," said Gerber, "that any target can be taken out, if you're willing to take the casualties and make the effort to do it. This proves what I've always said."

"I can get on the horn to Nha Trang and tell them the mission's a no-go under the current restrictions," Jorgenson offered.

"Shit," said Gerber, "I hate to reject a mission, because it makes us look chickenshit, but I can't see dying in a lost cause. Everyone agree with that?" When no one said a word, Gerber added, "Then, unless something else happens, we're going to pass on this. Let the Air Force do the job they're paid to do. A ground assault on a bridge that deep in enemy territory isn't something we can do with any reasonable certainty of success."

Jorgenson stood up. "Good. I'm glad you've seen the light. Sometimes, after so much effort has been expended, people tend to push on when it makes no sense."

"Sir," said Fetterman, "I learned a long time ago that sometimes it makes more sense to strike the colors than to sail on to certain death. Hell, it was a good mission into the North. We saw the bridge, captured an enemy soldier and got out with only the tiniest bit of incoming. I'm satisfied with that."

"Sergeant Teppler," said Jorgenson, "let's go scare up a jeep and get over to the TOC and see if we can confirm with Nha Trang."

"Yes, sir."

As the two of them left, Gerber stood up. "I think I'll catch some more sleep." He left the room.

MAXWELL LEARNED of the new development while working in his office. He sat at his desk, a can of Coke near his left hand. He was working on a secret briefing that would be given later in the day to the ambassador and his staff. When there was a knock on his door, he took a moment to put the report into the middle desk drawer and then yelled, "Come on in."

Pat, looking angry, entered, flopped into the worn visitor's chair and asked, "You know what those assholes have done now?"

Maxwell shrugged.

"First they ignore their orders and return, and now they say they aren't going in." Pat slammed a hand against the arm of the chair in rage. "Let our boys walk into a trap and do nothing about it. Well, it's not going to work."

"Excuse me, sir."

Pat faced Maxwell. "I said that they're not going to get away with it. I want you to go to Bien Hoa and order them to complete their mission. No shit from them. Their orders are to have that bridge down in ten days. Period."

"They're not going to take orders from us," said Maxwell.

"Maybe not, but they'll damn well take them from the Army. Orders will be issued through Nha Trang, telling them that a mission of no fewer than ten men will drop into the Thanh Hoa area for the express purpose of destroying the bridge."

Maxwell sat back and glanced at Pat. There was something else going on now. It wasn't that the bridge was that important, but the fact that Pat could order men into the field to destroy it. And it couldn't be just any men; it had to be specific men. Pat was proving just how much clout he carried.

"You sure this is a good idea?"

"The idea is sound," he snapped.

"Okay," said Maxwell. "What's the real reason for it?"

Pat sat quietly for a moment, then said, "It's not what you think. It's not even the bridge. It's the twelve men that went out before. They were thrown into the caldron, and the order to find them was ignored. Well, I've assembled a second team, real jungle fighters, and they're going in to search for the first team. I want their mission covered, and the bridge is the cover."

"Why not just have Gerber and Fetterman go back to look for them?"

Pat nodded. "I thought of that. I considered it, but then I didn't want them to be in a position to fuck this thing up. They might be willing to jump into North Vietnam again, but then they might just sit on their asses for a week pretending to search, claiming they found nothing. They won't get the chance to fuck me over again."

"This shouldn't be a personal vendetta," said Maxwell, "when lives are at stake."

"You're right," said Pat. "Men's lives are at stake. I've a dozen men out there somewhere, and no one has any idea where they are. I want them found."

Maxwell leaned forward, his elbows on his desk. He studied the snowdrift of papers there. There were unclassified reports about a hundred different things: the level of training of the ARVN forces, problems in the distribution system, assessments of the capabilities of the regional forces, the impact of network news on the war effort, and on and on. He studied the top sheets, his mind racing. "We could put a people sniffer up over the North," said Maxwell.

"For what? And how would we determine if we'd found the missing men or some NVA detachment practicing for war? I need men on the ground, and the attack on the bridge is the only way to do it."

"The men attacking the bridge are going to be cannon fodder."

"Not if they plan the mission right."

"Then let me tell them that it's a diversion for the real mission."

"No! They go in and they take out the bridge. As far as they know, that's the only thing they do. I want you to oversee that end of it, but don't tell them the real mission. You do, and it's your career."

"I know Gerber," said Maxwell. "He's going to work this out very carefully."

"Fine," said Pat. "You get him anything he wants. He asks for a B-52, you do everything in your power to get it for him. But you do not tell him, or anyone else, what's really going to happen."

"Yes, sir," said Maxwell.

"I'll be in and out to check on the progress of the men at Bien Hoa. I'll need to know exactly when they're going in so that I can make my arrangements."

"Yes, sir," repeated Maxwell.

Pat got up and walked to the door. He stopped and stared at Maxwell. "You tell them nothing, other than that they're going to destroy the bridge."

"Yes, sir." Maxwell watched the door close and then felt sick to his stomach. He'd had his differences with Gerber, but those had come about because of the nature of their jobs. He'd felt that they were friends, men who could trust each other. Now he found himself in the position of having to lie to his friend again. It wasn't something he liked doing. In fact, he hated it.

But then it was something he had to do. That was the nature of the job. Sometimes you just had to do things you didn't like.

JORGENSON RETURNED within an hour and kicked at the door. It swung open, slammed against the wall and fell off its flimsy hinges. He peeled the beret from his head and sailed it across the room where it struck the wall. The major whirled, put up both hands, twisted and punched a hole in the plywood.

Gerber, awakened by the noise, leaped into the room, a pistol in one hand. His body was covered with sweat from the late-morning heat. He was dressed only in OD boxer shorts and was wearing shower shoes. He took one look at Jorgenson. "Didn't go as planned, huh?"

"Made our report and was told to stand by. Word came down that we weren't allowed to abort the mission. It was a go and we had ten days to get it planned."

Gerber let down the hammer of the pistol and set it on the table closest to him. He rubbed both hands through his damp hair. "Then I guess we'd better come up with a plan that'll take out the bridge."

Jorgenson dropped into the nearest chair. "Have you got any ideas for a team on this?"

"We've what, five guys here? You, me, Fetterman, Teppler and Tyme. Need five others. A commo man, a medic and probably a couple of demo guys."

"At the very least," said Jorgenson.

"Whose our contact man?"

"Maxwell."

"Well, shit," said Gerber. He scratched his head. "He'll get us what we need and who we want if it's at all possible."

"Look, let's grab some lunch and then go over everything again with Teppler and Fetterman. We can decide if there's something we've overlooked that'll make this possible."

12

OUTSKIRTS OF HANOI
NORTH VIETNAM

On the drive into the village Phillips had seen bomb craters that ruined the symmetry of the rice paddies around them. They were huge things, at least twenty or thirty feet in diameter, and filled with water. As they passed a field that had four of them, Phillips used her 35 mm camera to record them. In the background, near a tree line of palms and deep green vegetation, a farmer walked behind a water buffalo. The picture sang with social relevance.

Once she had the pictures, she leaned back and closed her eyes. The heat washed over her, covering her with sweat. The wind rolling in through the windows did little to cool the passengers. High humidity was the culprit. Her hair was plastered to her forehead.

She opened her eyes and glanced at Travis, who looked pretty uncomfortable himself. His sport shirt was soaked and his hair hung down. He was staring out the window, one elbow propped on the edge, his chin cupped in his hand.

Nguyen sat in the front seat, staring out the windshield. He'd fallen silent since they'd reached the country. It was too hard to talk over the roar of the wind.

Phillips leaned forward and touched the Vietnamese on the shoulder. "How do we know the bomb damage was done by Americans?" she shouted.

Nguyen turned, an arm on the rear of the seat, and said, "South Vietnamese pilots refuse to fly into the North. Only the Americans are foolhardy enough to fly up here."

She nodded and sat back. They slowed then as the paved road turned into a rutted track leading off to the left. The driver followed it and they approached a village of mud hootches with thatched roofs. Pigs, chickens and a couple of puppies ran around in the dirt. The children, young boys and girls without clothes, stood to the side and watched as the car drove by. One girl raised a hand to wave.

They stopped in the center of the village. There were two bomb craters visible to the west, as well as the remains of a building. Broken brick, charred posts, bits of glass, smashed desks and chairs were strewn about. On a pole standing in front of the ruined building was a bell.

Nguyen pointed it out and said, "American bombs destroyed that school." He opened his door and got out. Turning, he reached for the handle to open the rear door for Phillips.

She swung her legs out and stood up. Holding a hand to her forehead, she shielded her eyes from the blazing tropical sun. Slowly she turned, taking in everything she could see. There didn't seem to be another building like the school in the whole village. Just mud and thatch. It certainly looked as if Americans were targeting schools.

The second car, which contained Young and Angstadt, pulled up behind them. Young was out immediately, trying to get his camera out of the trunk. Angstadt stood right behind him, waiting his turn. Both men were dressed in sweat-soaked one-piece jumpsuits. Neither looked happy about the assignment.

Phillips walked up to them. "I think we need to start with a panorama of the whole area. The mud huts and the people standing in front of them, then the bomb craters and school."

"What happened here?" asked Young.

"Once we get the area down on film, I'll find someone and we'll ask them on camera."

"We sure Americans are responsible?" asked Angstadt, finally getting at his gear.

"Who else?" Phillips sounded disgusted by the question.

Young put a case on the ground, flipped the locks and opened the top. He reached in, lifted out the battery pack and buckled it around his waist.

Phillips walked over to Nguyen. She blinked and surveyed the village. There were dirt pathways between the hootches where people walked. Other worn areas seemed to be the places where animals were staked. There was little green in the village. Pools of standing water stank like the open sewers of downtown Hanoi. The air was heavy with that odor, drifting from the rice paddies that surrounded them. She wanted to put a handkerchief over her nose, but didn't want to insult Nguyen or the villagers. "I'd like to talk to the people and find out what happened here."

"I can tell you that," said Nguyen.

"Makes no difference," she said. "I want the voice of a witness on film. You can translate for us, but I want someone who lives here telling me about it."

Travis came around his side of the car. "I'd like to get something out in the fields." He pointed at a group of people in a rice paddy, men, women, children, wearing coolie hats and shorts or pants rolled above the knee. Each was bent at the waist and clutched a bunch of small green rice plants. Behind them, another farmer was walking behind a water buffalo, a long switch in his hand.

"Yeah," said Phillips. "I see the point. People trying to earn a living just as they have for centuries, and then the Americans come in airplanes and drop bombs on them."

"Not exactly what I had in mind," said Travis.

Nguyen listened to them, then headed off while Young lifted a camera to his shoulder and walked over. Travis began giving him instructions, pointing to the various parts of the village he wanted filmed.

As Young began to shoot, Nguyen returned with two people. One was an old man with a long gray beard and a wrinkled face. Short and stooped, he wore a coolie hat, black shirt and black shorts. The other was a young woman, no more than twenty, maybe as young as fourteen. She was dressed in a rough silk shirt and black pajama bottoms. Her feet were clad in Ho Chi Minh sandals.

"You may ask them anything," said Nguyen. He didn't bother to introduce either person to Phillips.

Young had finished his background work and walked over. Angstadt was right behind him. "Now what?" Young asked.

"Let's get the people on camera," Phillips replied.

"Fine. How do you want to do it?"

Travis moved over. "How about this? You start on one of the huts, come around to the bomb craters and continue to the school. Carla can conduct the interviews in front of the school."

"That's an awful lot of motion. Won't be a real smooth transition," Young told him.

"If it doesn't work," said Travis, "we can fix it in editing. I just think it would be more dramatic if we could get it all together so that we don't have to cut it in."

"Where do you want me to stand?" Phillips asked.

Young glanced up at the sun. "About twenty feet to the left."

She moved to the spot. "Here?"

"Fine."

"If I could have the witnesses over here," she said.

When she had them all standing there, the girl closest, then the old man and finally Nguyen, just out of camera shot, she hoped, she said, "I'm ready."

Angstadt moved closer, the microphone in his hand extended. He held it up for Phillips.

Young got ready. "I'm rolling."

He focused on one hootch, then slowly widened his shot and began to move around. He stepped to the rear, got the bomb craters and then moved in so that he had the rubble of the school, finally tightening down until only Phillips and her two interviewees were visible. The rubble was behind them, softly out of focus, still there, still visible, a gentle reminder of where they were.

Phillips began her voice-over. "I am standing in a small village only a short distance from downtown Hanoi, the People's Republic of Vietnam. It's a primitive village where electricity is the magic of civilization and sanitary facilities don't exist. The people here scratch their living from the soil around them, living at the whim of nature, the elements and the American Air Force."

She paused dramatically, then looked at the two people with her. Pushing the microphone at the girl, she asked, "What is your name?"

The translation could be heard in the background. The girl looked at Nguyen as he translated, then told him, "Co Minh Dung."

"In your own words," asked Phillips, "can you tell us what happened to your school?"

Again the girl glanced at Nguyen and then began to speak. She spoke for nearly thirty seconds without stopping. Once she pointed to the right, where the bomb craters were, and then back at the flattened building.

When she fell silent, Nguyen said, "I was asleep in my bed when the airplanes came. We hear them often, but they just fly over. That night there came the sudden booms. They wake me and I am frightened. It sounds like the end of the world. I am afraid to move and pray the People's Defense can chase them away.

"There are many explosions and the air smells funny. Finally the noise stops and I go outside. There are many people outside, afraid. I hear crying and moaning and shouting. I come over here and see that the school has been destroyed."

Phillips nodded and asked the old man the same questions. The ritual was repeated. He had been greatly afraid, but had run outside to protect his family as best he could. The planes had finally gone away, leaving death and destruction behind them.

Phillips looked into the camera. "There was nothing in the village that would make a good military target. Just people who want to live their lives in peace. I'm Carla Phillips near Hanoi, North Vietnam." She looked at Young. "That's a wrap."

"Anything else you want?" asked the cameraman.

"Just grab some shots around here. Standard type stuff. If you see anything of real interest, let me know."

Young wandered off. Nguyen got the two Vietnamese out of the way. Travis walked up and said, "I'd like to get someone else to translate the girl's answer before we put it on the air."

Phillips took out a handkerchief and wiped her face, throat and neck with it. She grinned. "Did sort of sound like a propaganda speech, didn't it? The People's Defense, for Christ's sake."

"Easiest thing is to find someone at Berkeley to translate when we get home."

"I imagine," said Phillips, "we'll find, other than the propaganda phrases, that the translation was fairly accurate. Nguyen wouldn't go completely off on a tangent."

Young returned. "I think I've got everything we need."

"Then get your gear stored," said Travis.

Nguyen stepped up. "Is there anything else here you would like to see?"

"No," said Phillips. "I think that covers it."

"Then we'll go out to the crashed American jet. You'll see that we've made no false claims."

"I have no doubt about it," said Phillips as she got into the rear of the car.

GERBER PUSHED the map aside, then looked at Fetterman. "You know, Tony, if I didn't know any better, I'd tell Maxwell to have the Air Force bomb the bridge and we'd take out the antiaircraft sites. Give them a better chance of getting in and out that way."

Fetterman took a swig from a warm can of Coke. "Just how would you eliminate the air defenses, given that we've only got ten men and probably no more than thirty minutes to do it?"

Gerber rocked back in his chair, propped his feet on the table and laced his fingers behind his head. As he stared up at the ceiling fan and the parachute flare canopy that served as the ceiling, he said, "That's the easiest part. One man with one pistol can take out an entire SA-2 site. We get the radars and the sites are blind."

"Leaves the machine guns and the optically sighted weapons for the Air Force to dodge."

"So what? If they can't dodge a little poorly aimed gunfire, then they don't deserve their airplanes."

Suddenly Fetterman was excited. He sat up straighter and glanced at the maps and aerial photos. "The reason the Air Force hasn't gotten the bridge is because it's so heavily defended. We go in, knowing that the air raid is coming, quietly take out the radars, maybe string some plastique through the antiaircraft emplacements, and the Air Force doesn't have to twist and dodge. They can concentrate on dropping their bombs."

"Yeah," said Gerber, laughing. Then suddenly he understood that Fetterman no longer saw it as a joke. They didn't have to worry about taking six, seven hours to rig the bridge. They could literally throw the plastique at the guns, because any damage to them would be enough to take them out during the raid. Bend a barrel and the weapon would be worthless.

Gerber pulled the map over and looked at one of the aerial photographs. In it he could see part of an antiaircraft emplacement, gun barrels pointing at the sky. In one corner, almost completely obscured by the trees, was a truck park. Two vans sat side by side. They could be the radar vans controlling the weapons at the site. Easy to get to, a few explosives in the right place, and the guns they directed were useless.

He got another and another. In each picture there were shapes and shadows. When examined, they were clearly machine guns and antiaircraft artillery. He used a grease pencil to mark them and continued to work. Then he dropped his feet onto the floor and started sorting the pictures. "We need to get Justin in here and have him try to identify the sites. He should be more familiar with them than I am."

"Maybe we should call on Maxwell," said Fetterman. "If he isn't familiar with them, he'll get us someone who is."

"You really want to work with those CIA types after all the bullshit they've pulled on us?"

"Doesn't make the data they can give us any less valuable. They'll probably have better pictures."

Gerber stood, walked to the open door and looked out. A single jeep was parked in front of the hootch. The MP who guarded the gate was sitting in his hut, watching aircraft operating in the distance. "You're right, of course. Maxwell could be, probably is, the biggest asshole in history, but he'll have the information we need. We should tap the source."

"Yes, sir. No sense in ignoring the info just because we don't like the man."

"And he'll be a big help in coordinating the attack with the Air Force. It'd take us two weeks just to get permission to talk to someone about it."

Gerber returned to the table and sat down. Rather than look at the pictures, he said, "What we need is to decide how we want to do this and figure out the smallest number of men who can make it work." He tapped the map. "With an hour, I think five two-man teams could do it. Each team would have two, maybe three targets. That would mean we could take out between twenty and thirty of the radars and multibarreled weapons."

"I like this, sir. I like this better than trying to figure out a way to get six hours to rig the bridge. This has a chance of working."

"It puts the burden on the Air Force pukes to drop their bombs on target."

Fetterman nodded. "But I have faith in those boys. Take away the antiaircraft and they should be able to fly right down the pike. It's the difference between range shooting and combat shooting. When no one's shooting at you, you can concentrate on putting the rounds in the black ring."

Again Gerber stood up. He moved toward the door that led into their quarters. Stopping there for a moment, he turned. "You know, since we got the orders for this mission, this is the first time I've felt that we've got a chance of pulling this off."

"You think we can get the air assets to make it work?"

Gerber wiped a hand across his face, then looked at the sweat on it. "I think we'll be given anything we want as long as we can demonstrate the need for it."

"Then I think we've got a shot at pulling this off."

"Yeah," said Gerber. "Yeah, I think so, too."

13

HANOI

For three days Phillips and the news team were driven around Hanoi and its outlying districts. They saw, just as they had been promised, the wreckage of an American fighter-bomber shot down during a raid on Hanoi. They were allowed to film, photograph and touch it. They were shown its serial numbers so that they could prove it had been manufactured in the U.S. and bought by the American Air Force.

As they studied the plane, Phillips imagined what the feature on it would look like. Start with the plant where the plane was manufactured, go through the whole assembly process, maybe ask the workers how they felt about the product of their labors being used to kill Vietnamese women and children, and then find out where the plane had been sent. More film outside the base or whatever, and then finally, its resting place in North Vietnam. All that would make a dynamite feature of four to six minutes. More than the networks would have time to run, but a great showcase for her talent.

They saw how the Vietnamese were bearing up under the onslaught of American bombings. They took hundreds of feet of film with Vietnamese pointing at the sky, shouting their rage at Americans. They were told that America was so strong and that Vietnam was so poor. Why did the Americans want to destroy their tiny country?

It was a whirlwind of activity. They were served the Vietnamese breakfast of fish heads and rice cakes. They were given French food and American-style food. They went to a state dinner where North Vietnamese officials talked to them about the war and why the Vietnamese people would triumph in the end.

And finally, as they were walking down the street next to a canal that smelled worse than an open sewer, Phillips had the chance to ask about the strange round holes that were seen everywhere.

Nguyen stopped and said, "That's another result of the American bombing of our country."

Phillips stood in the late-afternoon sun, sweat staining her light blouse under her arms and down her front. She was getting tired of being hot, sweaty and sticky all the time. And she was getting tired of having to pull the information she wanted from Nguyen. He seemed to delight in making her ask question after question. "And what are they for?"

Nguyen nodded sagely. "When the air raid warnings sound and a person isn't close to a shelter, he or she may jump in here. It provides some protection for them."

Phillips walked over and looked into a hole. It was three, maybe four feet deep and just large enough for someone to crouch in. "I thought the U.S. wasn't bombing Hanoi itself."

"Miss Phillips, we've taken great pains to show you the damage in our capital. We've shown you damage in the city and just outside it. We've shown you wreckage of aircraft built in your country and flown by your countrymen. Do you believe that this is some sort of elaborate joke?"

"No," she said. "I'm only repeating what our President has told us repeatedly."

"I then suggest that your President isn't being completely honest with you. In fact, you yourself witnessed one of those raids the other night."

Phillips peered into the dark hole and thought about the terror of the people who hid in it. The air raid she'd witnessed hadn't been that frightening. She'd been awakened by distant booming, not unlike thunder drifting on a warm summer breeze. She'd sat up in bed and wondered if the rain would come soon.

A knock at her door surprised her. Nguyen whispered that she had to come with him. She scrambled into some clothes and followed the Vietnamese downstairs. They crossed the lobby and went down a narrow set of stairs into the dim glow of the basement. Everyone else was there, sitting on the floor. Lanterns burned.

The room itself looked almost like the interior of a prison cell. The rough concrete walls were painted flat white. A few old tables and a couple of chairs made up the furniture. Two wooden steps led down to the concrete floor. The air was cold and musty.

Travis stood and brushed at the seat of his pants. "Welcome," he said jovially, but his voice carried a hint of fear. He wasn't enjoying the raid.

"We're safe here," said Nguyen. "Even a direct hit wouldn't injure us."

Phillips made her way to one of the chairs and sat down. It creaked under her weight, but held.

Around her some of the Vietnamese talked in muffled tones, their voices singsonging rhythmically as they huddled together. She closed her eyes to block out the sight. It was too reminiscent of photos of Londoners crouching in subway tunnels while the entire Nazi air force tried to kill them.

In the distance she was sure she could hear the rumble of fighting—bombs detonating and antiaircraft guns popping, trying to bring down another American bomber. The sounds were faint, heard almost subliminally. Death rained from the skies, and it could claim her next. Sweat spread across her body, soaking her with fear. She wanted to get out and run, not sit still and wait, but there was no way to get out and nowhere to run to.

For what seemed like hours she sat there, her arms wrapped around her stomach as she leaned forward and prayed she wouldn't die. She tried to listen to the conversations, but the booming always seemed to intrude.

And then suddenly she realized she couldn't hear anything outside. Hoping the danger had passed, she said something about it, telling Nguyen that the bombing had stopped.

"That was the first wave," he had told her. "We'll wait to see if there's a second."

So they remained trapped in the claustrophobic room with dull white walls that threatened to fall on her. When there were no more sounds outside, she began to hope that the ordeal was over. And then, convinced that the Americans, her countrymen, weren't going to drop any bombs on her, she began to think. She searched the room and saw that Young was sitting against the wall, his head back and his eyes closed. "Tim. Tim, you got your camera gear?"

"Left it upstairs," he said without opening his eyes.

"I thought you cameramen never went anywhere without your equipment."

He opened his eyes and stared at her. "Except when bombers show up in the middle of the night and I'm told to flee for the shelter before I get killed. When that happens, I don't stumble around in the dark searching for a camera I might not live to use."

Now Phillips felt better. She believed she was going to survive the night. She looked over at Nguyen and asked, "Is it safe for my cameraman to gather his gear?"

"I think he would be completely safe."

"Tim, get your camera and return here so we can film a report."

Young got to his feet reluctantly. He stared at Phillips and then went to get his equipment. Fifteen minutes later Phillips finished a report, showing the Vietnamese crouching in the shelter, waiting for the raid to end. They sang what Nguyen described as patriotic songs, an activity that transformed them from a tired, irritable group into a spirited bunch defying the Americans. It made great television.

Phillips shook her head and shuddered at the memory of the air raid. Now, standing there and looking into a hole where people hid by themselves as bombs rained down, she felt the fear creep into her belly and spread outward. Sitting in a shelter with twenty or thirty other people had been pretty frightening. Crouching in a hole alone, however, had to be an experience that could cripple the mind. She felt sorry for the people who were forced to use the shelters, but she was also amazed at the simplicity of the design: a shallow hole available in case it was needed, just as if it had been a public rest room.

Phillips photographed one of the holes, backed up and took another shot showing a row of them. She retreated even farther, taking a picture showing the holes and part of the city in the background. Another great feature story, she thought. And this one would take only a minute to explain, which would ensure it network exposure. She'd show how the North Vietnamese coped with the possibility of an air raid at any moment.

Nguyen watched her photograph the holes. "We have much more to see."

She put the lens cap back on the camera. "Yes, of course." But she had to look back one more time at the holes and wonder how people could be so cruel to one another. If the American people knew what was happening to the North Vietnamese people, she was sure they would want to do something about it. But first they had to learn what the cost of war was.

IT WAS NECESSARY to break isolation. Although Maxwell had promised to get them everything they wanted, and although he had performed magnificently, Gerber knew the CIA man would have to meet the pilots personally. The coordination required for the mission was such that he wouldn't want to rely

on a third party to transmit messages between the Special
Forces men and the Air Force pilots.

Maxwell picked up Jorgenson, Gerber and Fetterman in a
jeep and then drove them to Tan Son Nhut. They didn't head
over to the SOG area, but turned along the flight line, stopping in front of a long, low building behind a series of fighter
revetments.

Fetterman hopped out of the back and stood on the tarmac,
looking at the building. Gerber joined him. It was hot on the
ramp, the sunlight reflecting off the corrugated tin that covered some of the revetments. The concrete around them
seemed to absorb the heat and radiate it back at them, making
it even hotter than usual.

Maxwell looped the chain through the steering wheel to
prevent it from being stolen, then said, "This way."

Jorgenson stood up. "Shit, it's hot."

They entered through a flimsy screen door whose hinges
squeaked. Inside, they found a narrow, dim hallway that was
even hotter than outside.

"I thought the Air Force was smarter than this," said Jorgenson.

They came to another door and stopped. A sign on it demanded that the door be kept closed. Maxwell opened it and
stepped back. The interior was bright and air-conditioned.
The cold air rolled out of the room.

"Hurry up," snapped one of the men inside, "before it gets
hot in here."

Everyone entered and Maxwell closed the door. He pointed
to the empty chairs around the conference table. "Take a
seat."

As they sat down, Gerber noticed that this was a conference
room that looked like all the other conference rooms he had
been in. There was a long, narrow table in the center surrounded by chairs. A pitcher of water and several glasses were
placed in the center of the table. Moisture beaded on the side
of the pitcher. The walls of the room were painted dull blue,
and there were several reproductions of fighters in flight on

them. One corner held an American flag. Another corner contained a screen. Opposite it was a slide projector on a small table. An Air Force sergeant in brand-new fatigues sat behind it, waiting for someone to tell him to turn it on.

The man at the head of the table stood up. "I'm Colonel Johnson." He pointed to his left. "This is Captain Kincaid, one of my flight leaders, and next to him is Captain Williams, my intelligence officer."

Maxwell introduced the Army men as everyone got into a chair. Once they were seated, Maxwell said, "I think I'll turn this over to Captain Gerber and let him explain the plan to you. Captain."

Gerber stood up and moved to the screen. He pulled a folded map from his pocket and used two paper clips to fasten the map to the screen. That done he surveyed the room. Finally he said, "We've been given a real son of a bitch of a mission."

"One that has the highest priority," added Maxwell quickly.

"Right," agreed Gerber. "Now I know that your men have been assigned the Thanh Hoa bridge, as have mine. Since you haven't been able to inflict any permanent damage, it's thought that a ground mission might do it."

"It's the antiaircraft around it," said Kincaid quietly.

"The reasons don't matter," said Gerber. "The point is, you haven't been able to take it out and the job has fallen to us." He could see that the Air Force men were ready to protest, so he lifted a hand to stop them. "We can't do it, either, not given the activity around it. Takes six, eight, ten hours to rig it to blow, and with four hundred North Vietnamese soldiers around it, well, it's impossible."

"Stalemate," said Johnson smugly.

"Well, sir," said Gerber, "that might be the case. Neither of us can destroy the bridge. You can't get the time you need over the target because of all the antiaircraft and we can't get the time we need because of all the enemy forces stationed there."

"Stalemate," repeated Johnson.

"No," said Gerber. "Not anymore. Working together, your men and mine, I think there might be a way that will take out the bridge without having to risk lives on an impossible mission."

Johnson suddenly looked interested. He glanced at Maxwell. "This have approval?"

"You agree to it and the mission's a go," said Maxwell.

"Okay, then, let's have it."

Gerber pointed to the map. "The major problem for the Air Force, as I understand it, has been the high concentration of antiaircraft fire in the region. While dodging that, it's difficult, maybe impossible, to make a good bombing run."

"Right."

"Then, to make a good attack, you'd like to see the antiaircraft defenses eliminated?"

"Exactly."

"All right. My proposal is to take in a small team and eliminate the radar facilities for those defenses. Granted, we can't get the optically sighted weapons, but we can damn sure take out the radar-controlled ones. When that's done, you'll have the time to hit the bridge with your bombs. Coordinating it this way, the bridge is down. My mission, impossible as it now stands, is complete, and your mission, impossible as it now stands, is complete. I just have to shift my target to something I can take out and provide you with the time you need."

Johnson sat there for a moment, his eyes focused on the map clipped to the screen. He glanced at Kincaid, then back at Gerber. "Are you sure you can take out the air defenses?"

Gerber rubbed his chin. "I'll need to get with your intelligence people to talk about it, but I think, given thirty, forty minutes, we can take out the majority of the weapons surrounding the bridge."

"If you can guarantee that," said Johnson, "I think I can guarantee we can drop the bridge. What's the time frame look like?"

"We've got about a week," said Gerber.

"Plenty of time." Johnson turned to Maxwell. "There a restriction on the ordnance we can carry?"

"Anything short of nuclear weapons will be fine."

"If we can get in," said Kincaid, "and lay a couple of thousand pounders into the right place, we can bring down the structure and destroy the foundation."

"Which is exactly what we need," said Gerber.

"I take it," said Maxwell, "that you have no trouble with the mission."

Johnson shook his head. "As long as it's fragged properly, I have no reason to refuse it. Seems to be a well-thought-out concept."

"Okay," said Gerber. "What we'll need to do is identify the targets for my men. You'll have to tell us what you want taken out, and then we'll have to work out a time frame to ensure that we've coordinated this properly."

"How long will you want to be on the ground?" Maxwell asked.

"I think," Gerber said, "that if we go in just after dusk, not National Guard nighttime, but after it's dark, we'd have a couple of hours to get to the bridge, another hour to eliminate the radar and destroy the guns, and the jets could hit the target at three or four in the morning."

"You won't be around when we start the bombing, will you?" asked Johnson.

"If your target is the bridge and we're not on it, then I don't see a problem."

"No, but I was thinking that we could give you a couple of extra hours. That way we could hit the bridge at first light. Naturally we'll be using our radar for target acquisition, but the daylight, even the little bit just at sunrise, makes it a better mission for us."

Gerber nodded. "We'll work out a timetable that suits everyone."

"I'll need a complete itinerary," said Maxwell.

"Why?"

"So we can coordinate with our other activities." He hesitated, looking sheepish, then added, "We don't want to accidentally compromise another mission."

"Oh, no," said Gerber. "The CIA would never do anything like that, would they?"

Maxwell ignored the question.

Johnson interrupted. "I suggest we get to work on this. There's not a lot of time before we have to have everything laid on."

"Of course," said Gerber. He returned to his seat. "I think we should work out the itinerary that Mr. Maxwell needs so badly. Major Jorgenson, Sergeant Fetterman and I will figure out the equipment lists, so we can have everything in place quickly."

"Oh," said Fetterman, "we're going to need another five to seven men."

"That's no problem," said Maxwell.

"Then let's get at it," Jorgenson said.

As the men bent to work, Maxwell got to his feet and left the conference room, knowing that everyone would be busy for the next few hours. That would give him enough time.

14

Maxwell worked it all out. Within days of the meeting at Tan Son Nhut, where everyone seemed to think they could easily take out the bridge if they coordinated their efforts, Maxwell knew the cover had been established. Pat dropped by his office and they talked about it. The senior CIA man wanted the new team on the same plane with Gerber, to let him know at that moment that he was being used as cover again.

"Don't do that," said Maxwell. "First of all, Gerber's mission is going to be noisy. You don't want the enemy to think anyone else is around. Use a second plane."

Pat thought about that and realized that they had the perfect cover. He could put his men in at dawn, as the air raids hit the bridge. It would give the team the chance they needed to get established.

"How long is your team going to be on the ground?" asked Maxwell.

"No more than two weeks. They told me that if you stay out longer, men become ragged, food begins to run low and the chances for a screwup get higher."

"Yeah," agreed Maxwell. "That's what Gerber's always saying. Where did you get these guys?"

Now Pat grinned. He was sitting in the single chair in Maxwell's office reserved for visitors, but he got up and began to pace. "Couldn't use Special Forces. Almost everyone in there knows everyone else. They keep such a close watch on those guys that I'd never be able to sneak a team into the North without everyone knowing about it. So I went to the LRRPs. Those guys are as good in the jungle as any you'll ever find."

"LRRPs are good," said Maxwell. "As are Marine Recon and the Navy's SEALs."

"SEALs are secret. No one knows about them. The Marines wouldn't have been a bad idea," said Pat. "Could have staged out of Da Nang."

Pat left right after that, after giving Maxwell a list of things he wanted done, as well as a file with a description of every man on the missing team. Pat wanted no screwups on that. If the search team found any American bodies, he wanted them to be able to identify the dead.

Maxwell arranged everything, using his office as cover. He got the two transport planes, one from the 505th Tactical Airlift Wing and the other from the 442d Tactical Airlift Wing. That was so that the pilots wouldn't be talking to each other and learning, accidentally, that they both had missions to the North on the same day.

He arranged to have Pat's LRRPs put into isolation at Ban Me Thout so that there would be no chance they would run into anyone from the Special Forces who knew about Gerber's team. He arranged for the equipment both teams would need, then sat back to wait for a chance to implement the plan.

The time before the mission melted away, and as it did, Maxwell began worrying about something Gerber had told him. The Special Forces Captain, annoyed by everything, had suggested that the security standards that kept the right hand from knowing what the left was doing sometimes did more to hurt missions than anything else. If he had known what the first CIA team was doing, he might have been in a position to render aid. The fact that he didn't know provided him with no opportunity to help. He couldn't plan for it.

Pat had been clear on that point. Gerber and Fetterman were not to learn of the existence of the LRRPs, or that they were going to search for the lost team. He had made it clear he didn't trust Gerber.

But the more Maxwell thought about it, the less he liked it. Gerber was the man who would be on the ground. If there was a chance the LRRP mission would affect his, he should be told about it. Petty jealousies had no place in the combat environment of Vietnam.

All morning he worried about it. At noon he made a decision: he would drive to Bien Hoa and tell Gerber that another team was going in to search for the missing men. That was the least he could do.

WHILE THEY WERE EATING lunch in the hotel, Nguyen announced, "We have a real treat for you. This afternoon we'll drive down the coast, look at a few of the fishing villages, then turn inland. We'll spend the night at a military installation, then head out to look at the Thanh Hoa bridge."

"What's so important about this bridge?" Phillips asked.

Nguyen put down his fork and smiled. He tented his fingers under his chin. "It's been attacked more often than almost any other location in our country, yet it still stands. The Americans have been able to do only superficial damage to it. It's a monument of sorts now."

"What kind of bridge?" Travis asked.

"A combination of railroad and highway. It spans the Song Ma, about seventy miles from the coast. It's a valuable link between the capital and our forces in the South."

"And we've . . . the Americans have attacked it repeatedly with no success?" Travis asked.

"That's correct. Many planes have tried to destroy it, but all have failed."

"Must be one hell of a bridge," said Travis.

"It was erected by Vietnamese engineers who have studied throughout the world. It proves we're not a backward, primitive people, but that we're able to construct modern bridges. We only need the chance and the opportunity."

"Sounds like it'll make a good feature," Phillips said. "I assume we'll be able to film there."

The smile left Nguyen's face briefly, but then returned. "Naturally we'll have to be careful of what's filmed, but there'll be an opportunity to do your job."

"And we're going to spend the night there?" asked Phillips.

"Certainly," responded Nguyen. "You'll have the opportunity to see some of our soldiers and observe for yourselves exactly how dedicated they are."

Phillips took a drink. "How soon do we leave?"

"After lunch. We'll take an hour or so to let our lunch settle, then we'll be on our way."

Phillips used her napkin to pat her lips. "Then I'm finished here." She slid back her chair and added, "I'm going to my room to rest for a little while."

Before any of the others could say a word, she left the room. She walked across the lobby and then up the stairs to the first floor. When she reached her room, she opened the door and entered. Before she lay down, she walked to the window and looked out at the scene that was becoming quite familiar to her.

North Vietnam was a country of contrasts—the primitive next to the modern. She had stood on the tarmac of a modern airport, next to the frontline fighter jets filled with the most modern electronics and avionics, and watched as a farmer wearing a coolie hat and black pajamas walked behind a water buffalo.

She turned and moved to the bed. As she sat down, she realized she was beginning to get used to the climate. It was always hot and humid. During the day it was hotter, but it never seemed to get cool.

As she lay back, there was a quiet knocking on the door. She glanced toward it and said, "Come on in."

Travis stuck his head in. "You okay?"

Phillips rolled onto her side and propped herself on her elbow. "I'm fine. I just wanted to get away from Nguyen and everyone for a moment."

"Yeah. I know what you mean." But rather than leaving, Travis entered all the way, shut the door behind him and leaned against it.

"They've kept us pretty busy the whole time we've been here," she said.

Travis moved into the room and sat down. He studied her for a moment, then said, "I'm a little concerned about the direction some of our reports have taken."

Now Phillips sat up. She stared back at him. "Everything I've reported is true. You know that as well as I do."

"Yes, but some truth is more true than other truth."

"What in hell kind of double-talk is that?"

Travis rubbed his face. "I'm just a little concerned that the picture we're painting isn't as accurate as it should be."

"Oh? And what's wrong with it?"

Now Travis scratched his head and stared at the floor. "I'm not sure, but I do know that it's not as one-sided as we're painting it. The poor North Vietnamese, harassed by Americans day and night. Villages attacked without warning. Schools and hospitals destroyed."

"You saw them," she said.

"I saw buildings that had been knocked down. I saw them surrounded by other buildings that haven't been damaged. I haven't seen an American plane in the sky the whole time we've been here."

"You were in the shelter that night. You heard the bombs dropping and the machine guns firing."

Travis was beginning to sweat. He got up and moved around. He glanced at the papers she had scattered on the table and then walked to the window. "I heard what Nguyen said were bombs dropping, but I don't know that they were bombs. It could have been artillery or even thunder. Hell, I'm not that familiar with the sound of falling bombs to be able to tell one explosion from another."

"You saw the school in that village."

"I saw a brick-and-steel building that had been destroyed. I saw a bell outside that was reminiscent of a school bell, but I didn't see any proof it was a school. Maybe it was some kind of factory that would have been a legitimate target."

"Oh, sure. You telling me we're so good we can select one building out of a village, bomb it and not hit anything else?"

"Are you saying we're so cold-blooded that we target only hospitals and schools, or that we're so bad we can only hit hospitals and schools?"

"Well..."

"And they've been very selective in what they've shown us. We're not allowed to roam unescorted. This has been a very cleverly managed tour. The impression of freedom while we're watched every minute."

"What are you saying?"

"That when we get back to San Francisco, we examine the film very closely. That we get someone who speaks Vietnamese to translate what's being said on camera. Make sure that Nguyen wasn't enhancing the translations."

"That would be fairly transparent."

"Of course," said Travis, turning. He looked at her and saw she was getting angry. He understood why. Here was the story of the decade, at least for her. Much better than covering the local scene, where she was required to attend city council meetings, or school board meetings, or maybe a fire. Now she was delving into something that was important. Something that could become a part of history, and the more controversial it was, the more likely that she would secure her place on the network and maybe in a few history books. Without the controversy, her stories would disappear, but if she could prove the government was less than candid, she would have something to make her name.

"What do you think we should be doing?" she asked.

Travis shrugged. "I don't know what more we could do here. Once we're back, maybe we should make arrangements to talk to someone at the Pentagon about the air war."

"So they can tell us national security is involved. If we talk to them, we won't be able to tell our story."

"That's not going to happen."

"You're damned right it's not. I've got my story. I know what it is. I've seen it all." She raised her voice. "You've seen the destruction yourself."

Travis felt his own blood pressure rise. "I'm saying that you're a little too ready to believe we're the bad guys in all this."

"Well, you don't see the North Vietnamese dropping bombs on San Francisco, do you?"

"A stupid argument," said Travis.

"Stupid, is it? I'll tell you stupid. Stupid is believing everything our President says without questioning it. Stupid is getting drawn into a war twelve thousand miles from home that won't affect us one way or the other."

Travis waved a hand. "Granted. But stupid is also believing everything the enemy, the *enemy*, for Christ's sake, tells you, no matter how open and revealing they seem to be."

"I'm smart enough to see through a sham and I'm smart enough to see the truth when it's laid out in front of me. Damn, Dick, I thought you were smart enough to see that, too."

Travis took a deep breath. "All I'm saying is that we'll have to evaluate the data carefully before we go on the air with it. We do have a duty to get it right."

"And we will. But we also have a duty to report what we see so that the American people can make their own decision about our involvement in this conflict."

"Okay," said Travis. "This wasn't the real reason I came up here, but that's not important now. We can talk about this in the studio in San Francisco."

"Fine," she said. She glanced at her watch. "When does Nguyen plan to leave for the bridge?"

"Twenty minutes or so."

"Time for a shower and change of clothes."

Travis almost asked if she wanted someone to wash her back, but then didn't. The argument was too fresh. He knew there were more fights to come. There would have to be, because he knew Phillips wouldn't take the unbiased, objective point of view in the stories. She would slide in her beliefs; he'd seen her do it before. Those other stories hadn't been that important, but now the stakes were much higher.

"I'll see you downstairs, then" was all he said.

"Fine."

GERBER HAD TO WALK out to the gate of the isolation area and vouch for Maxwell. The MP didn't recognize the CIA man, and his name didn't appear on the list of those who could be allowed in. Somehow no one had thought to add his name.

Gerber walked up slowly, stopped in front of the jeep and looked through the windshield at Maxwell. He then turned toward the MP, a young man in sweat-soaked fatigues who looked as if he wanted badly to be somewhere else.

"Mr. Maxwell can come in," said Gerber.

"Should his name be added to the list?"

Gerber's first intention was to say no, but knew the answer was wrong. Instead, he said, "Of course. He may be needed here again."

With that, he walked around to the passenger side and climbed in. The canvas seat was hot and nearly burned through his thin jungle fatigues.

As Maxwell ground the gears, trying to hit first, Gerber asked, "To what do we owe the pleasure of your visit?"

"Tell you and Jorgenson at the same time." As they stopped in front of the hootch, Maxwell asked, "Why wasn't my name on that access roster?"

"Who the hell knows, Jerry? I'm not the one who controls it, so don't go blaming me."

"Great. I spend two years in this hellhole trying to build a career and some dickhead decides I'm not important enough to have my name on some chickenshit roster."

"Jerry," said Gerber, "you sweat the small shit too much. Who the hell cares what some other asshole decides, unless it causes you real grief?"

Maxwell switched off the engine. "You're right, of course." He shook his head, as if to clear it of thought. "How are things progressing here?"

"Well," said Gerber, "we're as ready as we're ever going to be. The rest of the men arrived yesterday, bringing to twelve the number we have. Gives us one man to operate as jump-master and stay with the plane, a second to operate as a control, and the rest of us to go in."

"You're leaving two men behind?"

"They'll fill roles that we would like to have our men fill. That way we've got a little backup."

"Ten men going in, then."

"Just as we planned in the beginning."

"And the Air Force? Have they gotten everything set for their part of the mission?"

"Jerry, all they needed was the frag to get them on something official for the mission. They could have gone out the next day. Sure, they're ready. Now, I suggest we get out of the sun."

They got out and walked into the hootch. There were several men sitting around, cleaning equipment, guns and knives. Tyme sat on the floor in the corner, oiling a pair of new boots, working the toe and heel, trying to soften the leather.

"I'd like to talk to you and Jorgenson privately, if we can arrange it," Maxwell said.

Gerber clapped his hands once. "Men, take what you're doing somewhere else. Justin, find Major Jorgenson and get him in here."

"Yes, sir."

As the men cleared out, Gerber pulled out a chair and sat at the table. Leaning an elbow on it, he asked, "What's this all about?"

"We'll wait."

A moment later Jorgenson, wearing a sweat-stained OD T-shirt and fatigue pants, entered. He walked through to the dormitory area, then emerged, wiping his face with a towel.

Dropping into a chair, he asked, "What's so all-fired important?"

Tyme appeared and asked, "Anyone looking for something cold?"

Gerber checked the time. "It better be a Coke, given the schedule."

"Coke it is," said Tyme, and disappeared again.

Jorgenson threw his towel onto the floor. "Well?"

Maxwell looked at both men. "What I'm telling you is off the record. You can't repeat it to anyone, but I think you should be advised of the whole situation."

Before he could say more, Tyme was back with three cold cans of Coke. He gave one to each of the men and then left without a word.

Maxwell opened his can and drank deeply. The Coke seemed to affect him like whiskey, quickly refreshing him. Wiping his lips with his fingers, he said, "God, I needed that."

"Jerry," prompted Gerber.

"Right. I want you to know that another team is being sent in tonight, too. Their mission is to locate and rescue the first group."

Gerber snorted. "They better trained than the first group?"

"Army LRRPs," he said.

"They should be able to do it. They know about us?"

"Certainly. Everything you and your men are doing is a cover for that mission."

"If that's the case," said Jorgenson, "let's call it off right now and save some lives."

"Oh, no," said Maxwell. "I misspoke there. We want the bridge down. It has to be taken out, but the reason it has to be done so quickly is so that we can cover the second mission."

"We could have been asked to look for the other team, though I think we can tell you now what happened to them. The enemy eliminated them," said Gerber.

Maxwell picked up his Coke and drank again. "Doesn't matter. We've got to go look. I just wanted you to know there would be other Americans operating in the area."

Jorgenson slammed a fist into the arm of his chair. "I don't understand all this fucking around. It's almost as if you want to compromise our mission. Now where in hell are these fuckers going and when are they going in?"

"They're not going in until dawn, and a good twenty miles from your location. Shouldn't impact on your mission."

"That's something," said Jorgenson.

"Thanks, Jerry," said Gerber.

"Yeah, well," said Maxwell. He got to his feet. "Guess I'll head on back to Saigon. Oh, good luck on your mission tonight. I hope you put the whole bridge in the river."

"We're going to give it a shot," said Gerber.

Maxwell headed out the door, and as he did, Jorgenson asked Gerber, "You think this is going to hurt us?"

"No, but it sure could put the LRRPs into a bind unless the North Vietnamese know we've exfiltrated. We'll have to make enough noise getting out so the enemy won't be out searching for our guys."

"I guess we can do that."

"So," said Gerber, "I guess we better get to work."

15

ON A HIGHWAY OUTSIDE HANOI

Phillips was getting used to seeing the North Vietnamese countryside through the window of a car. As they traveled the highway, the landscape took on a redundant look. Rice paddies where farmers worked. Men and women, their pants rolled above the knee, walking through brown water, transplanting the rice shoots. Water buffalo being used to prepare the paddies for the rice. Then, in the distance, the lush dark green vegetation that marked pockets of jungle. Palm and coconut trees standing above tall bushes. Stands of bamboo, some of it a hundred feet high. Farmers' huts, mud walls and thatched roofs tucked into the small groves, using the jungle vegetation to protect them from the hot tropical sun.

And then there was the constant roar of wind as they sped along the highway. None of the cars they'd used had been airconditioned, as if that was a luxury the authorities refused. When most people in North Vietnam didn't have electric lights and indoor plumbing, it seemed wrong for government officials to have an air-conditioned car.

They drove east from Hanoi until they reached the port city of Haiphong. Nguyen allowed them to film ships at anchor in the harbor, demonstrating that support for their fight against the U.S. was worldwide. Neither Phillips nor Travis pointed out that all the ships were flying flags of Communist nations.

That done, they piled back into the car and drove south, near the coast where they could look out on the vastness of the South China Sea, a deep blue body of water where there were only a few fishing boats with the square sails of the Chinese junk.

They turned inland again, drove through farm country and out into open fields that stunned Phillips. She had been ready for the rice paddies, and for the rows and rows of rubber trees lined up with the precision of a military formation, but when they came to the corn, she was surprised. She hadn't expected to see corn growing in Vietnam.

Nguyen turned in his seat when she pointed out the fields. "We don't grow nearly as much as you Americans, but it's a crop that does well in our hot, wet climate."

"Can we get some pictures?" she asked.

Nguyen spoke to the driver, and he pulled to the side of the road. As they got out, a huge truck, painted a mottle green, roared by them. The men in the back waved and held up their weapons. It was the first time the news team had seen armed men in the country.

"Heading home for a leave," informed Nguyen.

Phillips nodded, but Travis asked, "How do you know?"

Nguyen smiled. "Have you ever seen soldiers happy when they were traveling in any direction other than home?"

"Good point."

Phillips told Young what she wanted, then watched as he dragged out the equipment. After making a few sweeps, he focused on a farmer as he walked out into his cornfield. While Young was filming, Phillips used her 35 mm camera to take a few pictures. Satisfied, she said she was ready to go.

They continued heading south, making good time because there wasn't a great deal of traffic on the road. They passed a military convoy that had been pulled to the side. The men sat in the shade of the trucks, sleeping, reading or writing letters. They didn't look up as the car drove by.

And there was the occasional oxcart, a huge thing with solid wooden wheels. Only a few pedestrians walked along the road. A young boy led a goat on a rope. Two women, both carrying heavy baskets. A couple of men.

Overhead the sky was clear of aircraft. During their stay in North Vietnam, they'd seen very few airplanes. Travis had questioned that, wondering where the American Air Force was, but Phillips figured they were hitting targets somewhere else in the country.

The drive took most of the afternoon. The road passed through a couple of small villages, but they didn't bother to stop. They drove through a couple of built-up towns that boasted a few stone and concrete buildings, many of them with definite French influence.

More people were visible in the towns. Banners hung from windows, and slogans were painted on the walls. Pictures of Lenin and Ho Chi Minh decorated these towns. And although they didn't stop, Phillips noticed holes in the sidewalk to protect the people from American air raids.

The thing that struck Phillips was that the Vietnamese people seemed no more concerned about the war than many of their American counterparts. People were going about their business and their lives without worrying about the war. The only time it came close was when the American jets flew over.

Finally they reached a built-up area surrounded by jungle. There were low buildings, tents, sandbagged bunkers, heavy machine guns and missiles. Everyone seemed to be wearing a uniform and carrying a weapon.

As the car slowed, Nguyen turned and looked over the back of his seat. "We're getting close to the Thanh Hoa bridge. It's guarded by an extensive air defense complex that includes the latest in sophisticated weaponry."

They turned off the main road and followed a dirt track. The car's tires kicked up a cloud of red dust that drifted with them. Soldiers watched them pass, but didn't seem too concerned. They finally stopped on a bluff overlooking the river valley. To one side was a huge sandbagged structure encircled by multibarreled weapons. Some men lounged in the late-afternoon sunlight close to the weapons. Off to the east, protected by the bluff, was an encampment of thirty or forty large tents.

Nguyen got out of the car and walked out on the bluff. A barbed wire fence marked its edge. When he saw that Phillips and Travis were with him, he pointed down at the bridge. "The Americans have tried to destroy the bridge many times. They have failed."

All around the bridge were military emplacements, guns and soldiers. To one side was a large yard that looked as if it belonged to a lumber company. Long rust-red I-beams were stacked in piles. Huge concrete and metal culverts, pallets filled with concrete and a series of small storage buildings baked in the afternoon heat. Vehicles, from trucks to cranes to bulldozers, were parked at one end of the yard.

"We're fully prepared to repair the bridge if it's damaged," Nguyen said. "The longest we've been without full service on it is only five days."

"Can we film from up here?" Phillips asked.

Nguyen folded his hands. "We would prefer you didn't. Our national security is at stake. We certainly wouldn't want to do anything that would give the Americans an unfair advantage."

"I understand," said Phillips.

"Tomorrow," said Nguyen, "we will be able to inspect the bridge and the emplacements around it. You will be allowed to take some photos and to interview some of the soldiers."

"And tonight?" asked Phillips.

"Ah, tonight, well, first we'll get you settled in. I'm afraid the accommodations won't be as luxurious as you've gotten used to in Hanoi. Dinner will be with the commander of this complex, and then I believe some sort of program has been arranged for entertainment."

"And we'll be allowed to film?" pressed Phillips.

"Of course. Tomorrow, after breakfast, you'll be allowed to tour the whole facility."

"Good."

LAWRENCE KINCAID, along with the other pilots, sat in the briefing room, the lights dimmed and the projector on. The intelligence officer, Captain Williams, stood on the dais, a pointer in hand, and said, "This will be the final briefing before the mission. The information given you is current as of 1500 hours this afternoon. As they say, this is the good stuff you're getting." The slide changed. "Tonight's target is the railroad and highway bridge at Thanh Hoa. Currently there are heavy antiaircraft emplacements around the target."

"Tell us about it," said one of the pilots.

There was a burst of laughter, and the intelligence officer grinned. "Well, give me a chance and I will."

"We know all about it," said the pilot.

"And what you don't know is that in ten hours most of those defenses won't exist."

There was a moment of complete silence. It was the first time in weeks that the intelligence officer had had their full, undivided attention. Then, suddenly, everyone was talking at once, shouting, yelling and pointing.

Williams stood there quietly, watching the turmoil he had caused. As they began to wind down, he said, "This mission is a combined operation with the Army's Green Berets. Those men will be airlifted into the area and will systematically destroy the antiaircraft defenses. By the time you hit the target, the only thing you'll have to worry about will be the 12.7s and a couple of optically sighted 23s."

Again the slide changed. "Approach on this one will be from the long axis, right down the bridge itself." He pointed at it and asked, "Now, any questions?"

"Just one," piped up one pilot. "How are these Sneaky Pete types going to eliminate all the air defense threats?"

"That's where the coordination comes in. They'll take out the radar vans, which will blind the defenders. Now it is possible for the missile commander to salvo his weapons, but without the initial radar guidance, it's going to be like shooting at you with telephone poles. Without guidance, it's going to be easy to avoid them."

"What's the window look like?"

"Given all the information we have, I don't think the window will be narrow. Time frame would be two to three hours."

"Where will the Sneaky Petes be during our raid?"

"They'll be off the site before you get there. If they aren't, then it's their problem. They've been briefed on the scheduling."

He waited, and when no one asked anything else, he said, "Thank you for your attention."

TWO DEUCE-AND-A-HALVES entered the isolation compound and stopped. Gerber stood in the doorway and watched as the drivers jockeyed around so they could back up to the hootch. Once they had done that, they stopped, turned off the engines and sat there, waiting.

Gerber turned and looked into the interior of the room. The men were all there, dressed in tiger-striped fatigues that had been manufactured in West Germany. Each man had an AK-47 rather than an American-made weapon. There were two reasons for that. One, if they lost a weapon, the enemy wouldn't be able to prove that Americans had been in the North. Two, it allowed the men to resupply from the enemy. The maps had been made in France and the pistols were from Belgium. Everything was from a foreign country.

None of the men had painted their faces yet. They would do that in the plane before they bailed out. The flight was long, and Gerber wanted them to have something to do, no matter how trivial it might be. With the review of the mission that would take place, he was sure he would be able to keep them busy for most of the flight.

He moved into the room and picked up the weapon he would be taking with him. Tyme, as he had done in the past, insisted that they indivdually zero their weapons. The rest of the equipment had been checked and double-checked. Fetterman had gone over the parachutes. Teppler and Jorgenson had checked the explosives. Hernandez and Bixel, two men brought in by Maxwell, were experts in communications; they had checked the radios. Like Tyme, Jones and Krupa were weapons experts, while Moxley would serve as medic. Luttell and Weiss would be left behind as controls.

The men picked up their gear and moved it to the waiting trucks. They piled it in, then climbed in after it. Weiss was detailed to go to Da Nang, and although he wouldn't be on the plane with the rest of the team, he climbed into one of the trucks with them.

Once everyone was loaded, Gerber and Fetterman made one final check of the hootch, determining that everything they had designated for the mission was gone. Luttell stood in the center of the room, looking forlorn.

"Cheer up," said Gerber. "Your job is to secure the beer for our return."

"How would you like to be left behind?" he asked.

"Someone has to do it, and you've had the luck of the draw," Fetterman said.

"Sure, Sergeant."

Gerber turned and stepped into the late-afternoon heat. He stood on the boardwalk for a moment, the diesel smell from the trucks overpowering him. The rumble of the engines was hard on the ears. He had wanted to say something else to Luttell, but the words just weren't there. What could you say to the man who was left behind?

Fetterman climbed into the back of the truck, and Gerber followed him. The captain leaned out the rear and shouted, "We're loaded. Let's go."

As Gerber sat down on the hard wooden bench, they moved out. Fetterman reached up and pulled down the canvas flap, wrapping them in darkness and heat. The sun baked the canvas. In seconds they were all bathed in sweat. It dripped down their faces and off their chins. Their uniforms were turned darker by the sweat, but no one said anything about the heat.

A few minutes later they stopped, backed up and stopped again. The driver turned and slapped the rear of the cab.

"We're here," he shouted, his voice nearly lost in the noise from the truck's engine and the sound boiling up from the airfield.

Fetterman lifted the canvas flap. They were backed up to the rear of a C-130 that had its ramp down. A man in a flight suit and helmet stood off to one side. A long black cord ran from his helmet to a connection at the side of the plane so that he could communicate with the pilots.

Gerber was the first out. He dropped to the ground, then hurried up the ramp. The rest of the men followed, tossing their equipment out as they exited. As soon as the truck was empty, it pulled away and the second took its place. When the plane was loaded, the loadmaster raised the rear ramp and pointed at the seats along the fuselage.

The men sat down and buckled themselves in. The interior of the plane, like the rear of the trucks, began to heat up rapidly. The momentary relief was gone as the pilots started the engines. As soon as the engines were running, the plane cooled off.

The loadmaster circulated among the men, making sure they were strapped in properly. He secured the equipment so it wouldn't shift in flight. When he was satisfied, he walked to the rear of the plane and sat down.

The noise from the engines increased, and they began to roll. They stopped once, the engines roaring, then began to move down the runway. The interior filled with sound as they bounced along faster and faster, then lifted off. The climb was steep, throwing the men toward the rear. There was a whine of servos as the landing gear retracted, and some of the buffeting stopped.

When they reached altitude, the noise in the rear of the plane quieted. Gerber unfastened his seat belt and crouched on the floor in front of the team. He took out the map they had made of the Thanh Hoa bridge area, including the air defense systems. Spreading the map out, he said, "One more review. The DZ is here. We can use the river for our route. Major Jorgenson and Sergeant Teppler will float down under the bridge, avoiding the lighted abutment near the center."

"You're sure we can do that?" Teppler asked.

"Yes," said Fetterman. "The lights are situated so that they play on the base of the abutment. The North Vietnamese aren't worried about people floating by, just those who might stop to drop off explosives."

Gerber took over again. "Once you're on the other side, you need to climb this hill and move north. You'll find a SAM site there. Aerial photos put the support equipment here, about half a klick from the SAMs. The radar control van will be obvious by the cables running to it. Cut the cables."

"Of course," said Teppler.

"The actual radar will be in an open area," Gerber continued. "If you can get to it, you can do more damage. Follow the cables to it."

Teppler and Jorgenson nodded.

"Once you've done that, you should have forty minutes to get to the next site. Same drill."

"Got it."

"When you've completed the mission, withdraw to the river and float down to the sandbars here." He indicated them on the map. They'd discussed exfiltration before. These sandbars were just short of the one Gerber and Fetterman had used earlier. Nothing got soldiers killed faster than using the same exfiltration point twice.

They went over the whole plan that way, Gerber briefing each team on its mission. Once that was finished, the men briefed it all back to him, explaining everything they would do. Gerber made sure everyone was aware of everyone else's mission and where they would be during the raid. The last thing he wanted was for two teams to shoot it out with each other.

That finished, they settled back. The loadmaster circulated among them, stopping to talk as the men checked their weapons again and again. Finally they spent time putting on the camouflage paint—green and black stripes to match the patterns on their fatigues and to hide the highlights on their faces and hands. When they were done, only their eyes and teeth weren't camouflaged, and they could take care of the teeth by keeping their mouths shut.

They continued the trip north, swinging out over the South China Sea. The sunlight that had been filling the windows faded and was replaced by darkness. Gerber moved to the rear of the plane and looked out. Far to the west he could see that the ground was still light. To the east the sea was dark, a few lights sparkling on its surface—ships patrolling the enemy's coast.

He returned to his seat and tried to relax, telling himself he had done all this before. Usually on trips into the North they tried to remain hidden from the enemy. This time they were going to move right into the middle of a major camp. Still, with a little luck, they would be able to get in and out before anyone knew they had been there, providing, of course, Maxwell hadn't lied about the other team. If the men were LRRPs, and if they were going in at dawn, they wouldn't affect Gerber's mission at all. If they went in earlier and fucked up, the entire North Vietnamese army could be looking for them.

He closed his eyes, trying to wipe out all the sound around him. He wanted to concentrate on something else for the moment, rather than think about the present mission. The planning had all been done, and now it was time to relax. He knew it was possible to overtrain or to get so worked up that mistakes were made. If he could hit that state where he was no longer concerned because it was just another mission, he would be able to sleep.

Fetterman had mastered the art. The man could sleep anywhere at any time. He didn't seem to worry about the upcoming mission. He went out and did the job without the pressure everyone else seemed to feel.

There had been a time, just after Fetterman arrived to become team sergeant, when Gerber had wanted to ask Fetterman about his ability. He'd thought about it, then decided against it; he'd already known the answer.

Fetterman would have said that he worried about the mission just as much as everyone else did. He would have said he felt the same pressures and fears. Gerber knew that, but there was something about the man that the captain respected, too. Something that suggested he wasn't just an ordinary combat soldier, but someone special. Someone who had the talent to become more than just a combat soldier. He was like a baseball player who didn't have to practice daily. He was so good that everything came naturally to him.

If Fetterman acknowledged that he felt the pressure, that he worried about the mission, that he was sometimes frightened by combat, he would somehow be diminished. So, intellectually, Gerber knew that Fetterman was like that, but he didn't want Fetterman to confirm it. He hadn't asked.

He pushed those thoughts from his mind and tried to relax. He must have succeeded because the next thing he knew Fetterman was touching his shoulder and leaning close to his ear.

"We've got to get ready," the master sergeant said.

Gerber was awake immediately, the sleep gone. He was ready.

16

MILITARY COMPOUND
AT THE THANH HOA
BRIDGE

The dinner hadn't been all that great, mostly rice with very little in the way of meat thrown in. Phillips had been afraid to ask what the meat was, fearing it might be monkey, water buffalo or, even worse, dog. It had tasted like chicken, so she had pretended that it was and had eaten her fill. There had also been water and wine to drink, neither of them very cold.

When dinner was over, they were taken out to look at the sunset, and the defenses manned by the North Vietnamese army. The men, and a few women scattered among them, looked dedicated and ready to do battle. They posed for pictures, many behind their weapons, which were pointed at the sky.

That finished, they moved back to a large tent whose side flaps were raised to catch the late-evening breeze. Chairs had been set up in rows and a small stage had been erected at the front. From the seats the audience could look at the stage as well as the Thanh Hoa bridge in the background. It made for an impressive sight.

Almost as soon as they had arrived, the rest of the seats were filled behind them. All the men sat quietly, waiting for the show to begin. Young and Angstadt set up the camera and sound equipment in an aisle off to the left.

After a moment, a man, dressed in a tailored uniform, walked to the center of the stage. He spoke quietly in Vietnamese for a moment, and the audience burst into applause. He waited, then said in English, "I would like to welcome our guests from the United States of America. We know the American people are a generous, kind people who wouldn't let the killing of innocent women and children continue if they knew what was happening. Tonight we hope to show you the people of what is called by your country, North Vietnam."

Travis leaned close to Phillips, who sat with a notebook in her lap. "Just like the Communists to use every opportunity to make a political statement."

"So what?" asked Phillips.

Travis shrugged. "So nothing."

The officer on the stage moved off to the left and held up one hand. As he did, a group of schoolchildren, boys dressed in black pajamas and girls wearing *ao dai*, marched to the center of the stage. They bowed once to acknowledge the Americans, then burst into song.

Their teacher stood to one side and translated the song the children sang. Her English was a little stiff, sometimes hard to understand, but the point of the lyrics came through. The song was about two lovers, a young man and woman separated by the outside world, which had created two Vietnams. The man and woman were separated by the cruelty of a world that refused to understand the Vietnamese people, who only wanted to live their lives without outsiders controlling them. It was a tragic story of young love broken apart by the cruelty of outsiders who cared nothing for the Vietnamese.

They finished the song, hesitated, then launched into another. This one called on every Vietnamese person to fight to bring all the people together and to throw off the yoke of foreign oppression. When they finished that song, to the wild applause of the audience, they bowed again and marched off the stage.

The officer came back and announced another performance. It went on like that as the sunlight faded and lanterns were lighted. There were no electric lights, all the electricity being diverted to the air defense complexes that ringed the bridge. No one seemed to notice the diminished light. They sat quietly, watching each act.

Phillips found it hot, humid and uncomfortable. She used her notebook to fan herself. The Vietnamese didn't seem to be affected by the heat.

Young used his battery pack to light the stage for his camera. He swept the audience several times, focusing on some of the Vietnamese soldiers. He lingered longest on a young woman, who was dressed in a khaki uniform, as were the men. Her long black hair hung down her back, and if someone had asked, Young would have guessed she was no more than fifteen. Next to her was her AK-47.

Finally the show ended. The officer who had introduced the acts thanked everyone for his or her attention and expressed the hope that the show had brought a little joy into their lives. The local school and the local farmers had wanted to show the soldiers that someone appreciated their sacrifice.

As the men filed out, Nguyen approached Phillips and said, "If you would like, the commandant has asked that you join him in his quarters."

Phillips looked at Travis, but Nguyen said, "It was a private invitation."

"I don't think that's a good idea," said Travis.

"Why not? I could interview him, talk about the morale of the troops and how they feel about having to defend their homeland from the Americans."

"In his quarters?" asked Travis.

"What could happen?" asked Phillips. "There are too many people here for it to be anything but innocent."

"Well," said Travis. "I'll be around."

As Travis left the tent, Nguyen steered Phillips in the other direction. The air was quiet as they walked along a path, and Phillips could hear the water in the river below them. It was almost as if the men had been told they had to remain silent in the camp—no loud talking, no radios, no horseplay.

They passed through the encampment, turned left and walked up a slight hill. The headquarters building, where the commandant waited, sat on the top. It was a small two-story brick structure with a flagpole in front of it, the only building of a permanent nature in the compound.

As they walked up to it, Nguyen said, "I'll stay for a while. The commandant's English isn't as good as it should be."

"Thank you."

Nguyen opened the door and they entered. The floor had the same kind of tile found on the floors of many public buildings in the United States. The walls were plywood, and there was very little furniture—a couple of desks, some chairs and a single bookcase. A huge picture of Ho Chi Minh covered one wall, while Lenin stared out from another. A rack of weapons stood under the Russian revolutionary's picture.

They passed through and walked up wooden stairs and into another hallway. At the far end light issued through a doorway and quiet music from a small radio could be heard. They found the commandant sitting behind a desk, working. To one side was a cot. The two windows in the room were open, and a fan stood near them, circulating air.

Nguyen shrugged. "In your Army there's a saying that rank has its privileges."

"But I figured in a classless society, such behavior wouldn't be tolerated."

"Except that while others are sleeping, eating, enjoying shows, the commandant is here, working. The privileges aren't a result of rank, but merely necessities so that he can work that much harder."

Phillips shrugged. "If you say so."

As they moved into the room, the commandant dropped his pen and stood to meet them. He didn't come around to shake hands, but bowed instead.

Nguyen said, "Miss Carla Phillips, may I present Colonel Minh Tran Giap."

Phillips bowed. "I am most happy to meet you, Colonel."

"And I you."

Nguyen hesitated, then asked, "Will you need me any longer, Colonel?"

In English the colonel said, "That will be all."

As Nguyen left, Phillips sat on the edge of the cot and got out her notebook. "Now, Colonel, if you don't mind, I have a few questions for you."

"Please," he said, grinning broadly.

EACH OF THE MEN in the rear of the C-130 moved to the pile of equipment that had been tied down in the center of the plane. They sorted through it, making sure each man took the equipment he was responsible for. Hernandez and Bixel picked up the radios and checked them carefully. Then they examined the URC-10s that each team would carry. Moxley went through the medical supplies, distributing small first-aid kits to each man. Teppler got out the C-4 and made sure everyone had some of it. They could stuff it in the barrels of the enemy's antiaircraft weapons. Although C-4 wouldn't detonate when the weapon was fired, it would cause a gun to blow up because of the obstruction in its barrel.

When each man had his equipment ready, his partner checked it out. They went through the whole routine as the loadmaster stood near the troop door and watched. As the plane continued on, he finally reached down and opened the door.

Luttell, who was acting as jumpmaster, told them to get up because they were getting close to the DZ. They hooked up and Gerber moved closer to the door. A step back from the opening, he looked out into the darkness of North Vietnam, just as he had done two weeks earlier.

For a moment everyone remained motionless as they waited to leap into space for a quick tumble to the ground. They wore only a main chute because they were jumping at such a low altitude that there would be no time for a reserve to deploy if the main chute failed to open.

Gerber stood there, his mind nearly blank. There wasn't much he wanted to see or think about at that moment. His static line was hooked to the cable, his equipment was strapped to him. All he had to do was step into space when the tiny light went from red to green and Luttell yelled "go."

"Thirty seconds," the jumpmaster bawled over the roar of the wind and engines.

Gerber centered himself and prepared to jump. Fetterman was right behind him. Jorgenson was the last man in the line, with Teppler standing in front of him.

Gerber kept his eyes on the little bulbs glowing in the troop door, waiting for them to change. Luttell stood close, one hand pressed to the headphones he wore. Then, almost before Gerber was ready, the light changed to green and Luttell shouted, "Go! Go! Go!"

Gerber stepped off into space and felt, almost immediately, the jerk as the chute opened. He glanced up at the canopy to see if it was fully deployed, then flexed his knees and kept his feet together. To the front he could see the dark line drawn across the horizon that showed him he was close to the ground. An instant later he hit and rolled. Coming up on his feet, he jerked at the shroud lines to collapse the chute. He hit the quick-release on his chest and felt part of the harness come loose. Shrugging his shoulders, he was out of the chute.

As the harness dropped away, he crouched and spun, listening to the jungle around him. The drone of the plane had faded and the only sounds were those of the men as they dropped into North Vietnam.

Fetterman came up behind him and leaned close. He kept his voice low, barely audible. "We're all down."

"Good. Take the point. I'll follow you."

Fetterman moved off then, heading due south. He entered a tree line and disappeared. Gerber picked up the pace and caught up to him. Fetterman was a vague shape, moving through the thick vegetation. As he entered the jungle, Gerber noticed that the air seemed to change. In the clearing of the DZ it had been cool and dry; now it was hot and humid as if the heat of the sun and the humidity from the river were trapped by the thick foliage. Sweat beaded on his forehead and dripped down his sides.

And now there was noise, too—insects buzzing, tiny claws scuttling across the jungle floor or up trees, water dripping as it filtered down from the triple canopy.

Behind him he heard almost nothing. Each of the men had been in the jungle before and knew how to move silently through it. They ducked under the vines and branches of trees. They put their feet down carefully, feeling their way along with toe and heel to make sure they didn't snap a twig or rustle the leaves. In the North there was no fear of booby traps as there was in the South. Because of that they could move a little faster.

As they did, Gerber felt the sweat soak his uniform. He wanted to stop for a drink from his canteen but refused to do so. It was only a mild inconvenience, and he knew the water would become precious before morning. He'd want a full canteen then.

Finally he heard the rush of the river. The odor in the jungle changed slightly. It was no longer a completely musty, rotting smell, but one that was underlaid with a certain fishy taint. The vegetation seemed to thin and he could see up into the night sky where stars were spread like sparkles on a black velvet blanket.

Fetterman stopped and pointed to a spot on the ground. Gerber moved to the spot and stopped. He held up a hand, signaling the man behind him that the patrol had halted. The message was relayed through the squad until each man had slipped into light cover.

Fetterman returned a moment later and whispered, "We've reached the river."

"Then we follow the bank."

"I make it a klick downstream to the bridge."

Gerber peeled the camouflage cover off his watch face and checked the time. "We've got three hours to get into position," he said.

Fetterman nodded, the motion exaggerated so that Gerber would be able to see it. He held a thumb up, then moved off again.

Gerber stood and waved to the rear as he followed Fetterman. They came out on the riverbank, then turned back into the jungle for twenty feet. Through gaps in the trees, bushes, ferns and vines, he could see the surface of the river shining—a quiet, dark surface that glistened with reflected starlight. Water splashed gently as it lapped at the bank or tried to tumble boulders from their positions.

As the men moved along, the background sounds of the jungle faded slightly. The bugs still buzzed and the lizards, monkeys and birds still called and scampered, but there seemed to be fewer of them. That meant they were closing in on the bridge. The animal life moved away from places where humans made their homes. For someone who knew that, it gave a clue about the number of humans in the vicinity.

Then, through the trees, came a faint flash of light—a single lantern inside the enemy camp. The light brightened for a moment, as if the person carrying it came closer, then it began to fade. Fetterman stopped the men, and they spread out in the jungle with great care.

Through the trees, Gerber spotted the abutment of the bridge. The searchlights were focused on its base, keeping swimmers away just as Fetterman had suspected.

Again Gerber checked the time. They were early, but he wasn't sure that mattered. The important point was that they needed to destroy the radar before the fighters arrived on the scene. The longer they had, the better the job they could do.

Jorgenson appeared and leaned in very close. "This it?"

Gerber nodded, but didn't speak.

"Then let's get going."

Again Gerber hesitated. Then he tapped Jorgenson on the arm and held up a hand, his fingers splayed wide, telling him to wait five minutes.

Jorgenson moved off and passed the word to the other men. Gerber crept closer to Fetterman and studied the layout in front of them. The ground seemed to slope down toward them. It was rough ground where the brush had once been cut back to give a clear killing field, but the bushes and grass had grown back. There was plenty of cover that led right up to the single barbed wire fence. It was obvious the North Vietnamese felt the only attack would come from the air. The fence was there to mark the boundary of the camp and not to keep Americans out.

The patrol quickly broke up into the teams that would attack the various sites. Fetterman moved south, along the fence, until he got close to the river. He hesitated there and looked up at the bridge. It was wrapped in darkness, and there was no sign of life on it.

He moved down toward the riverbank, using the thick vegetation as cover. Gerber followed Fetterman as he moved out under the bridge. They stayed away from a well-worn path, obviously used by soldiers when they wanted to swim or bathe in the river. The two Special Forces men worked their way under the bridge to the slope that led to higher ground on the other side. Once there, they stopped long enough to study the camp.

Again there had once been a killing ground, but it was now overgrown and useless. There were bushes scattered around, some of them four to five feet high. Beyond them, barely visible in the half-light from the stars, was an encampment. There were rows of tents in the center, a brick building close to the road on a slight hill, and a number of antiaircraft sites. Most of the latter contained ZSU-23s.

Fetterman moved east, skirting the fence and the overgrown killing field. They climbed the slope and came out on a slight rise that allowed them to look down into the camp. Surprised that the enemy hadn't put a guard shack, at the very least, on the hill, Gerber broke out his binoculars and studied the fortifications.

There wasn't much to see: dark shapes of tents, bunkers, gun emplacements, trucks parked at the rear of the camp, and two or three men moving, most likely guards.

Farther to the north Gerber could make out the raised berm that protected an SA-2 site. The captain turned and studied the area, checking to the east, where he thought he could see a group of trucks and vans parked under the trees. He tapped Fetterman on the shoulder and pointed. The master sergeant took the binoculars and checked it out. He nodded. Gerber took the binoculars back and put them away.

Fetterman moved off the hill, using it as a screen. They then fell back to the edge of the tree line, staying just inside of it.

It didn't take them long to reach the SAM site and skirt it. They stopped short of the truck park. A number of ZSU-23s were scattered around it as a ground-level to two-thousand-foot defense. Above that altitude, the SA-2s would be effective.

Fetterman leaned close. "How you want to do this?"

"Let's see if there are any guards, then crawl up and cut every damned cable we can find."

Fetterman stretched out so that the truck park was silhouetted against the sky. He kept his eyes open, watching and waiting. Finally he caught movement at the edge of the camp. He touched Gerber's arm and pointed.

"Yeah," said Gerber. "That'll be our first target." He pulled the camouflage cover off his watch, checked the time and added, "We go in two minutes."

Fetterman nodded, but didn't say anything. He was ready for the assault to begin.

17

NEAR THE THANH HOA
BRIDGE

Fetterman killed the guard. It was a simple thing to do. He waited until the man had walked past him, then rose from the cover at the edge of the truck park. Taking a single, unhurried step, he grabbed the man from behind. As he clasped a hand over the enemy's nose and mouth, lifting to expose the delicate flesh of the neck, the soldier tensed. Before he could react, Fetterman struck.

The razor-sharp knife whispered as it cut through skin and muscle. Blood spurted, and the air filled with the odor of hot copper. The NVA spasmed and kicked out as Fetterman brought the knife up from the rear, shoving it in under the rib cage to pierce the lungs and heart.

The copper smell was overpowered by the stench of bowels releasing. The enemy soldier groaned once, low in his throat, and went limp, dropping his weapon. As Fetterman stepped back, letting the body down gently, he glanced up and to the right.

The barrel of a second AK-47 was pointed right at his face. He hadn't seen the second guard come up, hadn't heard him, either. Before he could react, Gerber was there. The captain grabbed the enemy soldier's weapon, raising it sharply. There was a quiet pop as the Vietnamese's trigger finger broke.

As the man shifted weight, Gerber used the side of his foot. He brought it down sharply, then kicked again. The enemy released the rifle, and as he fell, he began to scream. Gerber punched once, a short jab to the throat. The NVA clutched his neck, and Gerber smashed the butt of the rifle into the man's face. The bones broke with a faint snap, not unlike the sound of someone pounding an overripe melon.

Fetterman moved quickly. He made sure the second man was dead, then crouched and peered at the camp. Now no one moved.

Gerber slung the AK over his shoulder and picked up the dead man. He carried him to the edge of the camp where the high grass would conceal the body. No one would find it unless he stumbled over it. Then, as Fetterman did the same, Gerber kept an eye on the camp.

When the bodies were hidden, Gerber pointed toward the radar vans. Fetterman moved off in their direction. He stayed low and used the available cover. Stopping at the corner of one of the vans, he waited until Gerber joined him.

The van was a Soviet-built ZIL with a canvas cover over the back. Wooden steps led up into the back. No light showed, and from the debris lying on the ground around it, Gerber figured it was a repair van.

Fetterman headed toward the second truck. Gerber stayed close behind. There was nothing in this one that interested them, either, and they moved on. Fetterman came to the third vehicle. Unlike the others, the rear was made of wood and there were three bundles of cables exiting from the door. When Fetterman spotted those, he turned, saw that the captain was watching and pointed. Then he lifted one of the bundles and grinned.

Gerber nodded and pulled out his knife. He grabbed one of the bundles and began whittling at it, as if it were a large chunk of wood. Rubber insulation, bits of wire and plastic peeled away as Gerber hacked at the cables. He leaned back against the side of the van and kept at it until the bundle broke in half.

As it did, he grabbed the second and cut through it. That done, he retreated toward the front of the truck and glanced right and left. Fifty feet away was one of the ZSU-23s—a twin-barreled weapon that took a crew of three. One man sat in the seat while the other two kept the ammo flowing and helped the gunner turn the weapon. Gerber peeled off a small piece of C-4 and jammed it into the barrel.

Finished, he returned to the van. Fetterman had moved on to the next vehicle, in the line, where he was cutting through another bundle of cables. Gerber leapfrogged past him to the last truck. It was another of the repair vehicles. He used some of the C-4 to plug the tail pipe, hoping it would ruin the engine when the enemy tried to start it.

Fetterman joined him there and whispered, "That should do it."

Gerber stood next to the last van and felt drained. They had been at it for fifteen minutes, but it seemed like hours. He was sweat-soaked and needed a drink of water. He glanced at his watch. "Time to get another."

Fetterman didn't hesitate. "Let's do it."

THE INTERVIEW had gone well. Phillips found the commandant articulate, intelligent and friendly. Some of his attitudes were old-world, probably a French influence, but he had also been well indoctrinated by the Communists.

He had sat at his desk during most of the interview, listening to the questions and then carefully, haltingly, forming his answers. When he sensed Phillips had run out of questions, he stood up and unbuckled his Sam Browne belt. Dropping it onto his desk chair, he smiled. "Some wine, perhaps?"

Phillips was taken aback by the sudden shift. One minute she was a journalist and he an officer in a foreign army, the next she was a woman and he a man. Phillips wasn't sure she liked the change. She certainly didn't like the feeling that she had lost control of the situation. "Wine?" she echoed. "I don't think so."

"A small one, as a symbol of mutual respect." He didn't wait for her reply, but moved to a small cabinet behind his desk and took out a bottle and two glasses.

Phillips got to her feet quickly. "No, really, I should be going. I have some work to finish."

"But this will only take a moment," said the commandant. "A single, quick drink."

"There are others waiting for me, and I still have work to do tonight."

"Our French friends often said that all work and no play make Jacques a dull boy."

As the man advanced on her, Phillips retreated slightly, but found herself trapped. The door was behind the commandant, who was already trying to unzip his pants. Phillips couldn't believe she'd allowed herself to get trapped in this situation. She had taken the North Vietnamese at face value, assuming that all of them were gentlemen, just as Nguyen had been. Now, out in the field where the men hadn't seen all that many women, she found that the commandant had taken her journalistic interest as some kind of romantic overture.

"I really must be going," she said, a slight quaver in her voice.

"The night is young," said the commandant. "Very young, and no one will miss you." He moved closer.

"This isn't right."

"The People's Army needs all the support it can get, and you have offered support."

Phillips continued to retreat, bumping into a wall. "I offered no support. I'm here to cover a story."

"So now you have the opportunity to lend support. Not everyone is as privileged as you."

Phillips realized she wasn't going to be able to talk her way out of the mess. The commandant had the attitude that all women were on earth for him to use, or not use, as he decided. He didn't think he was doing anything wrong; he was just taking what was rightfully his.

Phillips knew she could submit, let him have his way and get it over with, or she could fight. Submitting just wasn't something she found easy to do. She had the right to pick her partners, and if she wasn't attracted to a man, she shouldn't have him overrule her.

So she smiled at the commandant and saw that the ploy worked. He let his hands drop to his sides and then straightened. The tension drained from him, and he smiled. "I see you have come to your senses."

"Exactly," she said. She let him come near, and when he was in range, she stepped close and shoved him as hard as she could.

The commandant, taken by surprise, stumbled backward until he hit his cot and fell over, hard. His head snapped back and banged the wall with a loud, solid thunk.

As that happened, Phillips ran to the door. She threw it open, then turned to look at the commandant. He was half lying, half sitting on the cot, rubbing the back of his head.

"So you want to play?" he said, his voice husky.

Phillips didn't want to play at all. She ran down the hall and stopped at the stairs. For a moment she hesitated, but then saw the commandant's silhouette in the doorway. She rushed down the stairs, turned and ran to the front of the building. Opening the door, she stepped out into the night.

As she entered the open compound, she realized she wouldn't be safe until she reached her own people. The commandant would run her down, and with the help of his soldiers, drag her back. Once she reached Travis and Nguyen, the game would be over. But not until then.

JORGENSON CROUCHED near a large bush covered with huge foul-smelling flowers and watched as two men talked. The hand of one glowed orange because of the cigarette he held. Jorgenson could smell the burning tobacco on the light breeze that blew his way.

Teppler was off to the left, lying on the ground, watching the same two men, who were supposed to be walking guard. He had slung his rifle and drawn his knife, waiting for them to separate so that they could be taken.

The enemy soldiers laughed loudly, and the smoker took a last puff. He flipped the cigarette away, and it landed in a miniature explosion of orange sparks that faded quickly. With that, he turned and moved east.

As he did, Jorgenson was up and moving. He reached the barbed wire fence and dropped to the ground. On his back, he lifted the bottom strand, which had almost no tension in it, and slithered under. Once clear, he rolled onto his stomach and glanced at his man, a dark shape walking slowly away.

He came up on his hands and knees and shot a glance to the rear. Teppler was closing on his man. Knowing that his back was covered, Jorgenson moved rapidly. He reached the enemy in two large steps just as the man was about to turn. He slashed with his knife and felt it cut through the flesh of the throat. There was a faint whispering, like someone tearing silk gently.

The man grunted in surprise and pain. Both hands came up to grab at his throat. He dropped to his knees with a thump, turning his eyes upward, to look at Jorgenson. The major moved in and jammed his knife into the man's chest under the sternum. He felt the blood flow, covering his hand with hot, sticky liquid.

The enemy soldier grunted quietly and fell backward, doubling his legs under him. He sat halfway up, then collapsed. As he did, the knife jerked from Jorgenson's hand. The major crouched, pulled his knife free, then wiped the bloody blade on the dead man's pants.

That done he returned his knife to its scabbard and picked up the dead man's weapon. He pushed the thumb release on the back of the breech, pulled the top of the weapon off and dropped it onto the ground. Then he stripped the bolt and pocketed it. He let the trigger mechanism fall into his hand and pitched it underhand into the grass just outside the wire. Jorgenson didn't like leaving a functioning weapon behind if he could help it.

Teppler joined him then, carrying the AK he'd taken from the body of the man he'd killed. When he crouched next to the major, Jorgenson touched his arm and pointed at the truck park not far away.

"Right," said Teppler.

Jorgenson loped off, bent at the waist, trying to keep low. He reached the front of one of the trucks and stopped. Teppler worked his way past that truck and halted at the second. The major leapfrogged beyond him, then stopped. He spotted the cables and dropped to his knees. While Teppler kept watch, Jorgenson used his knife to chop through one bundle of wires and then a second.

Satisfied that they had crippled the radar, they began a quick retreat. They moved east, where the ground dropped away and the jungle was closest to the wire. Crossing the wire, they dropped into the grass, listening to the sounds from the camp. No one seemed concerned that two guards had disappeared.

TYME AND HERNANDEZ worked their way through the maze of antiaircraft weapons quickly. Although Tyme had wanted to stuff C-4 into the breech of each weapon, he was afraid someone might notice the obstruction, so he contented himself with stuffing some of it down each barrel.

While he stood in front of the first weapon, Hernandez sat in the gunner's seat and lowered the barrel so that Tyme could reach it. The sergeant stuffed the C-4 in and Hernandez raised the barrel again. Finished, they moved to the next weapon in the line and repeated the process. They avoided the ZSU-23/4s because they were radar-guided, which meant they were the responsibility of other teams.

When they came to the 12.7s, which were little more than heavy machine guns, they plugged their barrels, too. The idea was to sabotage anything that could throw a round into the air. They moved quickly, quietly, avoiding trouble by taking cover whenever anyone came close.

The enemy was easy to avoid. They didn't expect a raid on their camp, so they weren't alert. They went through the motions of guarding their camp, but didn't expect any trouble. That allowed Tyme and Hernandez to work uninterrupted.

When they finished one side of the camp, they turned, and in the darkness, saw a black shape that Tyme recognized as the Spoon Rest radar, used by SAMs for target acquisition. Tyme couldn't pass it up, even knowing that other teams were taking out the radar vans. He stopped and set a charge on it, timed to explode at sunrise. If the coordination was good, it would destroy itself about the time the fighters were crossing the North Vietnamese coast.

Hernandez guarded Tyme as he worked. Then, together, they moved off toward another area packed with ZSUs. They had plenty of time to take out more of the antiaircraft weapons before they had to return to the river for exfiltration.

JONES AND KRUPA moved through the enemy camp easily. There were no guards anywhere. They came to a vehicle park that looked like one of those used by the command posts for the SAM and other antiaircraft sites, but as they searched, they learned that it was abandoned. It was really a motor pool or a "boneyard" where parts were stripped to be used in trucks and vans that were still running.

They worked their way through it carefully, watching for signs of the enemy, but found nothing. There were no guards and no mechanics. It was as if no one cared what happened to the trucks. Krupa stopped near one of them and opened the gas tank. He could smell the diesel fuel in it, meaning no one had thought to drain the tank to conserve the fuel.

If the enemy was going to be that sloppy, Krupa decided they should be punished. Taking a grenade, he wrapped it in a thin rubber strap, making sure the safety handle was held down securely. That done, he pulled the pin and dropped the grenade into the fuel tank of the truck. In three or four days the diesel fuel would destroy the rubber, the safety handle would pop and the truck would blow. Long after they were gone.

Finished, they moved on, doing what quiet damage they could, but finding nothing extraordinary. Unhappy with that, they retreated, falling back toward the river, figuring to get into position with Bixel and Moxley, who were holding the exfiltration route.

They left the camp, stopped at the wire and waited, but no one followed them. They lay in the grass and watched the camp. From somewhere they could hear singing, not the drunken singing of men who'd spent too much time in the club drinking beer, but the songs of men who had nothing else to do and were passing the time.

Satisfied that they had been in the camp and gotten out without anyone knowing it, Krupa got up. Keeping his head low, he worked his way toward the jungle. When he reached it, he stopped and waited until Jones caught up to him. In the morning the enemy would be able to see their paths through the thick, thigh-high grass, but at night their trail was invisible.

When Jones joined him, Krupa began to work his way south toward the river. Now that they were back in the jungle, it was suddenly hotter and wetter. They kept moving, avoiding the trails that would have let them run toward the river. Instead, they hiked through the vegetation, trying to avoid the vines that ripped at their clothes and exposed skin. They dodged around the trees and bushes, moving stealthily.

Jones used his compass, taking readings every fifty yards, making sure they hadn't gotten turned around by the dense vegetation. There was no noise from the camp, just the rustling of leaves above them as the breeze tried to find a way down into the thick jungle to blow away the heat and humidity.

They stopped once to rest. Krupa drank some of the water he carried, then gave the canteen to Jones, who drank gratefully. Krupa was tempted to finish off the water so that it wouldn't slosh around in the canteen as he moved, but the wind was picking up. The trees overhead rattled, as if a storm was coming up. He doubted the enemy would hear the almost inaudible slosh of the water with the noise that nature was making. Besides, there didn't seem to be any enemy patrols around them.

They moved off carefully, with Jones holding his compass in one hand. He turned right, stopped, then started again. For a moment he walked straight, then stopped once more. He glanced right and left and sank to one knee.

Krupa reached Jones and leaned close so that his lips were only a fraction of an inch from his partner's ear. "What in hell's the problem?"

"We should be there."

Krupa turned and crouched, his spine pressing against Jones's. He searched the blackened jungle around him. There was nothing to see other than the shapes of bushes, ferns, clumps of grass and hanging vines. The wind caused everything to shift and shake, but nowhere around him could he spot anything that resembled the exfiltration route. He leaned his head back so that it was nearly resting on Jones's shoulder. "We should be there."

"Yeah. They have to be around here somewhere."

Just as they were about to get up and move east, a voice came out of the dark. "Shut up before you give us all away."

Grinning, Krupa whispered, "Looks like we found them."

PHILLIPS TURNED AND RAN across the open ground in front of the headquarters, away from the encampment and away from where Nguyen, Travis and her camera team waited for her. She'd lost her sense of direction, wanting only to put distance between herself and the demented commandant.

She slipped once and fell heavily. Feeling a pain in her side, she rolled over onto her hands and knees. As she glanced to the right, she saw the commandant hurrying toward her. He probably sensed victory.

Before she could scramble to her feet, she saw a second shape to the left—a tall, thin man, not small like all the Vietnamese she had seen. He had to be an American. Thinking that Travis or Young had gone for a walk, she leaped up and ran toward the shape, shouting, "Dick! I'm here, Dick!"

The figure froze and turned to look at her.

Now the commandant was closer, maybe twenty feet behind her. As she slowed, he did the same thing.

"The commandant had some ideas about the relationship that I didn't share," she told the still-indistinct shape.

"Your friend will be of no help to you," said the commandant.

Phillips spun. "Why not?"

The enemy officer stopped and stared into the darkness. There was very little light. What there was came from the stars or the scattered lanterns that glowed throughout the camp. He pointed and said, "Because he is not a military officer, and I command here."

Phillips turned. "You'll have to stop him, Dick."

"I'm not Dick," said Gerber.

18

TAN SON NHUT
SAIGON

Kincaid sat in the passenger seat of the jeep, one foot on the dash, and looked out over the airfield. There was a multicolored glow from the lights on the runway, taxiway and various ramps. A jet engine whined somewhere out of sight, and a single helicopter hovered over the airfield like a moth around a flame.

Johnson hugged the wheel. "Intel says the Green Berets are on the ground and moving toward the target. Radio contact has been established and maintained, so the assumption is that everything is on schedule."

"All right," said Kincaid, "my only question is, do we attack under every circumstance?"

"If you mean, is the attack on even if you get SAM warnings, the answer is yes. Are you expected to make perfect runs, the answer is no. But the mission is on."

"Yes, sir."

Johnson sat back and closed his eyes. He wiped the sweat from his forehead. "You'll know, long before you get there, whether or not the Green Berets were successful. If they failed, then your failure to drop the bridge will be understandable." He opened his eyes and looked at Kincaid.

"And if they're successful, the bridge had better end up in the river."

"Larry, you don't want to make us look bad, do you?"

"No, sir."

"This mission's a dream. We have the Army coming to *us* to help them out. We're needed to complete their mission. Now, if they succeed in setting up the conditions for us, we can't fail. Who knows when they'll ask again."

"You can count on me, sir."

"I am."

"Yes, sir. I had my chance earlier and I missed. The reason I missed was the enemy antiaircraft. With that gone, we'll be able to put everything right on the bridge."

"I know it," said Johnson. He glanced at his watch. Insects buzzed around him. Sweat dripped down his sides. Again he closed his eyes. "There's not much else to say now except, good luck. I know there's a pep talk I should give you, but damn, I'm not up to it."

Kincaid laughed. "You don't think I deserve a pep talk before this mission?"

"I'm not sure you need one. Hell, man, just drop the fucking bridge and I'll buy the beer."

Kincaid lifted himself out of the jeep. He turned and grabbed his flight bag from the back. "You've got yourself a deal."

He started off toward the revetment where his jet fighter was parked. The crew chief stood beside it, silhouetted against the lights at one end. A ladder leaned against the fuselage and an APU sat near the nose. They were taking no chances.

Johnson watched as Kincaid nodded to the crew chief, handed him the flight bag and climbed up the ladder. Just before he stepped into the cockpit, he turned and waved. Johnson waved back, then started the jeep. He backed up, turned and drove toward the operations building. Once there, he turned off the engine, but didn't get out. He sat in the jeep and watched as Kincaid started his plane and moved out onto the taxiway. The flight of four joined and rolled out together.

Although it would have been cooler inside, and he could have listened in on the plane-to-plane conversations, he was happy to sit where he was. He could see the planes and he knew what was being said—the same things that were always said.

The aircraft moved along the taxiway, the flames from the engines bright in the night. They all stopped at the edge of the runway, then moved toward it. Kincaid, in the lead aircraft, took the runway first, followed by his wingman. The second element held short. A moment later the first two jets began to roll, the flame from the rear longer and brighter. The sound built to a deafening roar as the jets lifted from the runway, flew parallel to it for a moment, then rotated, climbing out rapidly.

When they lifted from the runway, the second element took its position and the routine was repeated. The planes then disappeared into the darkness west of Saigon before heading north. The engine noise faded, and for the first time that night, it was silent at Tan Son Nhut. Nothing was landing or taking off.

Johnson started the jeep and turned the wheel. He decided to find a cup of coffee, then catch a couple hours of sleep. It would be that long before the jets hit the bridge, and he wanted to listen in to the radio chatter once the attack began.

THE COMMANDANT LOOKED at Gerber and then at Phillips. His teeth seemed to gleam when he smiled. "Back off and you will not get hurt."

"Please," said Phillips.

Gerber stared at the commandant, wondering what had happened to Fetterman. The master sergeant had undoubtedly taken cover somewhere close. Gerber had to take the commandant quietly so that an alarm wasn't raised.

Slowly the commandant advanced. At first he said nothing, then in halting English he warned, "You go away and you will not be hurt. Go now."

Phillips retreated, moving so that Gerber was between her and the colonel. She had no idea who the newcomer was or where he had come from.

Gerber stood his ground, and as the commandant got closer, he realized the newcomer was someone who shouldn't be there. He stopped moving and demanded, "Who are you?"

Gerber lifted his hands, as if to surrender, then moved in. He struck once, the edge of his hand slamming into the throat of the enemy soldier. The man gasped as his head fell forward and he collapsed. He rolled onto his back, his hands clutching his throat, clawing at his neck. Gerber used his knife, killing him quickly.

"What in hell did you do that for?" Phillips cried.

Gerber stood and spun. "Shut up."

"You didn't have to kill him."

"I did," said Gerber. "Now, what in hell are you doing here?"

Phillips was too stunned to speak. She looked down at the body of the commandant and then up at Gerber.

"Captain, we've got to move," Fetterman whispered from the darkness.

Phillips spun and stared. "How many of you are there?"

Gerber knew that each second they stood there the chances of someone seeing them increased. Still, he hesitated. He had no idea who the woman was or why she was on the enemy's base.

"Captain," hissed Fetterman.

Gerber shrugged and moved to the left. He joined Fetterman, and both of them ran toward the edge of the camp. As they reached the wire, they stopped. Gerber looked back and saw that the woman was still standing over the body of the dead man.

"We'd better get out."

There was a single shout and a light stabbed out. The body of the dead man was illuminated. Three men ran toward it while the woman stood there as if unable to move.

As Gerber slipped under the wire, he saw the woman point at him. One of the men froze, then waved an arm. All three began running toward the edge of the camp.

"We take 'em, Captain?"

"No choice."

Fetterman and Gerber separated, staying low and using the tall grass and bushes for concealment. Gerber crouched and slipped back under the wire as two of the men came closer. They were chattering in Vietnamese, their voices high, strained, as if afraid they'd find something or someone.

One of them came up and put his hands on the top strand of wire. His partner stopped short, staring into the night. The third man diverted to the south, near where Fetterman hid.

Gerber rose out of the grass and grabbed the man farthest from the wire. With one hand under the man's chin and the other on the back of his head, Gerber snapped his hands to the right. There was a quiet sound, like gravel being crushed in a bag, and the man sagged.

As the second man turned, Gerber kicked out as if attempting a fifty-yard field goal. The enemy soldier started to shriek as he collapsed to the ground.

Fetterman took his man with a knife—a single, strong cut that nearly severed the head from the body. The enemy guard went down as if his bones had suddenly melted. He never made a sound.

But the woman they had left behind did. She screamed, her voice rising like a siren in the night. There was shouting from around the camp and more lights came on.

Gerber leaped over the fence, using one of the poles, his hands on top of it. He crouched in the grass and pulled his rifle from his shoulder.

Fetterman joined him. "There was something about that guy."

"What?"

"Something about that guy," repeated Fetterman.

A shot was fired. Gerber saw the muzzle-flash off to the right. The bullet didn't come close.

"Time to get out," he said. He turned and began to crawl away. Now a siren did begin to wail, and more lights snapped on. There were only a few of them—small searchlights that crisscrossed, looking for the disturbance. One of them focused on the bodies and was joined by the others. Men began running across the compound, two of them breaking off to stop near the woman.

Firing erupted all around them. The night sparkled suddenly as if fireflies had gotten loose. A couple of rounds snapped overhead, but the rest were fired at shadows.

Gerber reached the trees and stopped. He stood up, shielded by a huge teak, and looked back at the enemy camp. There was shouting and shooting and sirens from all over. Men were pouring out of their tents in various states of undress. Most carried their weapons, though they were confused, unsure of what to do or where to go.

Suddenly there was more firing. One of the heavy machine guns began to chug, the tracers flashing into the night and bouncing high.

Fetterman touched Gerber's sleeve. "We'd better get going."

As he turned there was a quiet explosion and then another, as someone tried to use the booby-trapped weapons.

"Shit," said Gerber.

He turned, and with Fetterman, worked his way deeper into the jungle. As the firing faded in the rear, Fetterman said, "They'll probably put out patrols now."

"We'll just have to avoid them."

They took off, running through the jungle, back toward the rendezvous point. As they moved, they could hear the shouting and firing from the camp. The siren continued to wail, but it didn't seem that anyone was inclined to give chase.

As the sounds from the camp faded away, they slowed. Fetterman checked his compass, then moved off toward the east. Gerber brought up the rear, moving carefully, listening for the sounds of a pursuit that never developed.

Fetterman came to the river and turned again, backtracking slightly. Within minutes they found the rest of the team. They moved up carefully and learned that everyone had now returned. There had been no casualties, though it had been interesting.

Gerber checked his watch. "Then let's get the hell out of here."

Before they could move, Fetterman was next to Gerber, leaning close. "Remember I told you that there was something that bothered me about that guard."

"Yeah."

"He was wearing an arm band."

"So?"

"I've seen it before, on our first trip in here," said Fetterman.

Gerber was about to say something, then stopped. "You don't mean..."

"Yes, sir. He was wearing one of the arm bands the missing team had on."

"Jesus, we've got to tell Maxwell to stop the LRRPs. They don't need to jump in here, not if the NVA has the arm bands. The other team is dead."

"Or captured."

"Same thing." Gerber moved off to find either Hernandez or Bixel. They were responsible for the long-range communications. He had to tell them that they needed to get Net Control and cancel the LRRP mission.

Hernandez listened as Gerber told him what he wanted. "Now?" was all he asked.

"As soon as you can. We've got to get that mission stopped."

"Yes, sir."

But then Tyme was there. "Sir, sounds like we've got visitors. Someone moving in the jungle."

"Shit. Let's get out of here. You take the point and head, more or less, toward the extraction point."

"Yes, sir."

"And let's hurry it up. We've got to make radio contact with Net Control."

"Yes, sir."

Tyme took off into the jungle, moving southeast. The rest of the team spread out, trying to put distance between themselves and the enemy camp.

PHILLIPS STOOD near the body of the dead commandant and watched as the soldiers ran toward her. She didn't move and didn't put her hands over her head. She still wasn't sure what had happened or who had done what.

One of the Vietnamese was shouting at her, but she couldn't understand a word. During her brief stay, she'd picked up a couple of Vietnamese phrases, but none of them covered this situation.

Then, out of the darkness, Nguyen was there. He glanced at the body of the commandant. "What has happened?"

Phillips didn't move, didn't take her eyes off the dead man. "I...he...I..." She shook herself. "The commandant seemed to think I would go to bed with him. Seemed very insistent about it."

"And?"

"I ran out and he chased me. There was . . ." She stopped and glanced to the rear, where the American had disappeared. Suddenly the war was no longer an abstract thing being fought by people she didn't know. Suddenly it was all brought home to her. It was a real conflict between people she had spoken to.

"What happened?" asked Nguyen again.

"I don't know. A man was here and I ran toward him."

"What man?"

"I don't know. A man. The commandant seemed to know him." She knew that was a lie, but then there wasn't anyone around to argue with her. "They spoke and then fought."

"You mean this man killed the commandant."

"Of course," said Phillips. "Then he ran away." She turned and pointed at the fence. There was no sense in lying about it. The three bodies there showed that something had happened.

Travis appeared then. He ran up with two Vietnamese. Travis had on his khaki pants and had stuck his feet into his shoes but hadn't bothered to lace them. "What in hell's going on?"

Phillips stood her ground. "The commandant tried to rape me and a man killed him."

"Rape? A man? What the fuck?" Then he stopped to think. "Are you okay?"

"I'm fine."

"Miss Phillips," Nguyen said, "we must find the man who killed the commandant."

"Why? He was helping me."

"He killed an officer of the People's Army. Soldiers cannot take discipline into their own hands."

"He was protecting me."

A man appeared from the gloom and spoke to Nguyen. When he finished, Nguyen asked, "Can you describe the man who killed the commandant?"

She hesitated, then shook her head. "It was too dark and I didn't get too close. After he...killed the commandant he ran away."

Travis looked at Nguyen. "I think we'd better get out of here."

"In the morning..."

Travis checked the time. "It's only thirty minutes to sunup," he said. "Let's just make plans to get out now."

"I'm afraid we'll have to wait. There are men in the field now, searching for the intruders."

"Who said anything about intruders?" asked Travis. "I thought it was some kind of internal problem."

"There are reports," said Nguyen. "Men may have attacked the camp and the commandant was killed because of it. Please. We will leave in the morning, but not for a few hours."

Travis grabbed Phillips by the hand and announced, "We're going to our quarters then."

"Please," said Nguyen, "return to your quarters. I shall come over there in a few minutes and we'll make our plans."

Travis pulled at Phillips until she followed him. They walked across the compound. To the east the sky was beginning to pale and the stars fade. When they were out of earshot, Travis asked, "Now what in hell happened?"

Phillips shrugged. "I don't know. The commandant was trying to get into my pants and I fled. Out here I ran into a man who killed the commandant and then disappeared into the night."

"Did the man speak to you?"

"Yes. He wanted to know what in hell I was doing here."

That stopped Travis for a moment. He looked at her. "Now why would he want to know that?"

"I think he was an American."

For an instant Travis didn't believe what he had heard. Then suddenly it dawned on him. "I think maybe we'd better get the hell out of here as fast as we can."

THE GROUP HAD NO TROUBLE reaching the rendezvous point. Travel through the light jungle near the river's edge was simple. Tyme kept the pace steady, and the noise they'd heard when they'd started faded into the background. The enemy wouldn't be able to mount a thorough search until daylight, and by then they should be busy with the Air Force.

Once they reached the exfiltration site, they spread out and formed a loose defensive ring. Hernandez, with one of the large Angry-109s, worked to get his antenna rigged. He used the keypad and tried to raise Net Control in Nha Trang. For a moment it seemed as if he wasn't going to have any luck, then suddenly he got an answer.

While Gerber stood over him, he informed Net Control to contact Maxwell in Saigon and call off the LRRP mission. He repeated that twice and was acknowledged. He then requested that the exfiltration choppers be dispatched. They were ready to get out.

When he got acknowledgment, he shut down and began breaking down the set. Gerber, satisfied that the message had been received, moved away. Fetterman appeared and leaned close. "No sign that anyone knows we're here."

"Good. With luck we'll be gone before they realize we were here."

"Who was the woman?" he asked.

Gerber shook his head. "Damned if I know. My guess would be some kind of journalist doing a story on the North Vietnamese and how the war affects them."

"That's what we need," said Fetterman, "some damned journalist in the North telling everyone what a lousy, cruel, terrible thing we're doing by fighting the war."

Gerber couldn't think of a thing to say to that. Instead, he asked, "We ready to go?"

"Once the choppers get here, we'll be ready."

Hernandez came up and said, "Choppers are inbound. Be here in just a few minutes."

"We get this coordinated right," said Gerber, "and the Air Force can help cover our exfiltration."

Then, from the east, came the rumble of jet engines and the pop of light antiaircraft defenses. Fetterman looked at his watch. "Air Force is right on time."

"Let's hope their luck is as good as ours."

KINCAID LED THE FLIGHT over the North Vietnamese coast, veered west, then turned north. Below him the ground was just beginning to brighten with the first hint of the new day. Again he turned and saw the target in the distance—indistinct grays and blacks that were almost impossible to see. Then, suddenly, as if someone had turned on a light, he saw the bridge laid out in front of him like a model on a table.

Kincaid glanced at his instruments and saw that there were no warnings. The SAMs were down. The radars were down. Nothing was showing on his threat display. In fact, no one was even shooting at him yet.

He eased the stick over and rolled to the right slightly, lining himself up on the bridge. He could see it in front of him, a long, narrow line only fifty, sixty feet wide, but plenty long. Suddenly he knew everything was going to work out.

As he watched, the first stream of tracers came up at him, a thin green line off to the right. He grinned into his oxygen mask and again checked the threats. None of the radars had shown yet.

Firing below became thicker. More weapons shooting, more tracers climbing slowly toward him, but all of them off to the right or left. Small-caliber weapons. Finally a single ZSU opened up, the rounds from it looking almost like basketballs as they floated skyward, but still the aiming was poor.

Glancing out of the cockpit, Kincaid saw that the flight had spread out for the attack. He would lead them in, one at a time. The last aircraft would take pictures as well as drop bombs. With luck, there would be very little for that one to bomb.

Kincaid lined up on the bridge and began the dive toward the target. He seemed to fall out of the sky as the enemy started to fill the air with tracers. More weapons shooting, but still nothing from the big guns or from the SAM sites that ringed the bridge.

Kincaid was suddenly relaxed. Machine guns didn't scare him, especially machine guns that were optically sighted. A lucky bullet could kill him, but that was an everyday chance. It was the SAM missiles that chased you as you tried to break away that scared him. It was the SAM missiles that made it hard to concentrate on aiming the bombs because you had to keep one eye on the threat panel. But that threat was gone. Eliminated by the men on the ground.

He dived at the bridge, saw that everything was lined up the way he wanted it, then touched the button that released his bombs. It had taken the flipping of fourteen different switches as they had crossed the North Vietnamese coast to allow him to release the bombs so easily. He'd had to set it all up before he had started the run at the bridge. But that done, he had been able to drop the bombs the instant everything was set.

As the bombs fell from his aircraft, he pulled up. While he climbed rapidly, he twisted around, trying to see behind him. He pushed the stick to the right to give him a better view.

The first bomb was on line, but fell short, hitting the railroad track that led to the bridge. The second was on target. Kincaid saw the explosion on the bridge before it was obscured by the smoke, dirt and debris. Satisfied, he eased the climb and started his turn to the east, slowing so that the rest of the flight could catch up to him after they had dropped their bombs.

He leveled out and glanced to the rear. The whole length of the bridge seemed to be wrapped in smoke and fire. A lot of people were running around, but there wasn't much shooting.

"Yeah," he screamed into the oxygen mask. "Yeah." He wanted to do a barrel roll, but didn't. Instead, he keyed the mike and said, "Rover flight check."

"Two joined."

"Three joined."

"Four to your six o'clock, but closing."

"Stretching it out," said Kincaid. He hesitated, but couldn't wait. "How did it look?"

"Fucking beautiful" came the reply. "Spans are down and in the river. Looks like we fucked it up real good."

Kincaid knew that wasn't the kind of report that should have been made, but it spoke to him eloquently. "Roger. Let's head for the barn."

As he added power, racing toward the safety of the South China Sea, he risked a final glance to the rear. There was nothing to see except a rising cloud of smoke and dirt from the destruction of the bridge.

EPILOGUE

Everyone who had been involved in the mission to the North sat in the briefing room waiting for Captain Williams, the intelligence officer, to let them know if it had been a success or failure. Gerber, along with the other Special Forces men, sat in the back two rows. The Air Force pilots and their ground crews sat in the front. Colonel Johnson stood behind the podium while Williams hovered at his elbow.

Before anyone said a word, Gerber knew that some of the mission had been a success. Net Control in Nha Trang had gotten a message to Maxwell, and he had canceled the LRRP mission. Fetterman's discovery of the distinctive arm bands that had been worn by the missing team had been enough; Maxwell convinced his boss that the team was dead.

There had been a quick debriefing about that, along with a more detailed one concerning the defenses at Thanh Hoa and the weapons systems deployed. When the debriefing was over, Gerber had asked about the American woman at the camp, but was told that it was none of his business. The State Department was fully cognizant of the woman's presence, and it had been approved at the highest levels of government.

Fetterman had suggested what the highest levels of government could do, but Gerber had gotten him out of the room be fore anyone said anything that would get them all into trouble. Now they were at Tan Son Nhut, waiting for the BDA.

A slide came up and Colonel Johnson said, "Okay, here we go. Before I let Captain Williams have the podium, I'd just like to say that I've been impressed with the way this joint mission went. I hope we can arrange more of them in the future. Now, Captain Williams."

The intelligence officer took his place at the podium and then turned, pointing at the picture. "As you can see, the entire structure of the bridge is involved here. Damage runs from one end to the other."

The next picture came up. Although there was a great deal of dust and smoke in the way, it was easy to see that the first span of the railroad bridge was down. As Williams pointed that out, there was a cheer from the Air Force pilots.

"Yeah," shouted Kincaid. "Got the son of a bitch."

Williams flipped through the pictures quickly. They could see that the damage wasn't limited to the one span. Other parts of the bridge were missing. Railroad track, twisted out of shape, flashed in the early-morning sun. Parts of the highway bridge blocked the river. Fires were burning on both sides of the river and both sides of the tracks and highway. Thick smoke obscured the camps around the bridge.

Williams signaled the projectionist and the last slide faded from sight. He moved to the center of the stage and said, "Estimates are that the bridge will be out of commission for six to eight months. That's if there is a concentrated effort to restore it. If not, a year, maybe two. The only thing we don't know is how badly the abutments were damaged. That could change the estimates."

"Meaning?" shouted one of the Air Force pilots.

"Meaning that if they were damaged, too, add a year, maybe two to the repair estimate. If not, then the six-month figure will probably stand."

Gerber leaned over and said to Fetterman, "Not the best results, but we all got out alive. Can't argue with that."

"No, sir, you sure can't."

HALF A WORLD AWAY Travis sat at the head of the table in the conference room and looked over the script that lay in front of him. There were a couple of film canisters on the table. Phillips sat opposite him, one hand holding a copy of the script.

"I don't like this," said Travis.

"It's a great story. We know there are Americans operating in North Vietnam because I saw them. Two of them at least."

"I don't know," said Travis.

"I see them and an hour later bombs are falling all around us."

Travis grinned. "The bombs didn't fall all around us. Just on the bridge. Amazingly all the bombs fell on the bridge except for the one that hit the tracks on the south side of it."

"Still, the story is the fact that there were Americans in North Vietnam."

Travis leaned back in his chair. "I think what we should do is concentrate on the other information we got."

"I think we should consider the other story."

Travis shook his head. "I don't want to have to overrule you on it, but I'm afraid that if we let that information out, if we report it, we might accidentally endanger other men operating in North Vietnam."

"Even when our own government lies to us about it, claims there are no ground operations in the North."

"Well, that just makes good sense. If they acknowledge those operations, then the enemy is going to be alerted to them. This is one of those times when national security—"

"It's not national security," snapped Phillips.

"Right," agreed Travis, "not national security. One of those times when the premature release of the information might endanger American lives."

Now Phillips sat forward, her elbows on the table. "But if we release the information, tell the public what's happening, maybe we can stop the missions. That would save lives, too, both Vietnamese and American."

"We're not in the business of making policy. That should be left to the men and women who have all the information and who can make intelligent decisions."

"Jesus, Dick, what bullshit. It's our responsibility to hold those people accountable. If we don't, then they can do anything they want. Who's going to challenge them?"

"I'm very uncomfortable with this whole story." He tapped the cans of film. "I think this is one that we should voluntarily withhold."

"No."

"At least until we can get a better feeling for what's going on in the North."

"You saw as much as I did."

"Yes, and I don't agree with all your interpretations of the facts, but that's something we can argue about later. I just want to sit on this other story. You don't need it."

Phillips nodded slowly, then said, "I never said I needed it. Hell, there are very few stories that a reporter needs. But when a good one falls into your lap, you can't ignore it."

Travis stood up and walked around the back of his chair. He sat down again and said, "If the American hadn't been in North Vietnam, at the bridge, you know what would have happened."

Phillips snorted once. It was a sound that was a cross between a laugh and a cough. "I was waiting for you to pull that one out."

"And I'll add one other thing. How many civilians were hurt in that raid, or in the air attack that followed?"

Now Phillips was quiet. She stared at the tabletop for a long time. When she looked up, she said, "No one else has this story."

"Right," said Travis. "That's why we can sit on it for a while. We can check on it because no one else has it."

She lowered her eyes again. She thought of the look in the commandant's eyes as he had tried to catch her, and then as he had chased her across the dark compound. She thought of his words as he'd told her there was no one around to help her.

His men would help him, but not her. Then she thought of the unknown American who had literally dropped from the sky to help her when she had needed it. He had taken care of the problem and then run off. He'd asked her for nothing.

But that didn't mean she owed him nothing. He could have easily escaped into the night without stopping to render assistance, but he hadn't. He could have stayed hidden in the dark, but he hadn't, and now she owed him something whether she liked it or not. Whether she agreed with what he did or not. Finally she looked up at Travis. "Okay. We kill the story."

"We can always run it later, after the war," said Travis.

"Sure," she said. "If anyone will want to see it then, as if it will make a difference then."

"Maybe the important thing is that it makes a difference now," said Travis.

"Maybe," she agreed, but she wasn't sure.

GLOSSARY

AC—Aircraft commander. The pilot in charge of an aircraft.

ADO—A detachment's area of operations.

AFVN—Armed Forces radio and television network in Vietnam. Army PFC Pat Sajak was probably the most memorable of AFVN's DJs with his loud and long, "GOOOOOOOOOOOOD MORNing, Vietnam!" The spinning Wheel of Fortune gives no clues as to his whereabouts today.

AIT—Advanced Individual Training. The school a soldier attended after Basic.

AK-47—Assault rifle usually used by the North Vietnamese and Vietcong.

ANGRY-109—AN-109, the radio used by the Special Forces for long-range communications.

AO—Area of Operations.

AO DAI—Long dresslike garment, split up the sides and worn over pants.

AP ROUNDS—Armor-piercing ammunition.

APU—Auxiliary Power Unit. An outside source of power used to start aircraft engines.

ARC LIGHT—Term used for a B-52 bombing mission. It was also known as heavy arty.

ARVN—Army of the Republic of Vietnam. A South Vietnamese soldier. Also known as Marvin Arvin.

ASA—Army Security Agency.

AST—Control officer between the men in isolation and the outside world. He is responsible for taking care of all problems.

AUTOVON—Army phone system that allows soldiers on one base to call another base, bypassing the civilian phone system.

BDA—Bomb Damage Assessment. The official report on how well the bombing mission went.

BISCUIT—C-rations.

BODY COUNT—Number of enemy killed, wounded or captured during an operation. Used by Saigon and Washington as a means of measuring progress of the war.

BOOM BOOM—Term used by Vietnamese prostitutes to sell their product.

BOONDOGGLE—Any military operation that hasn't been completely thought out. An operation that is ridiculous.

BOONIE HAT—Soft cap worn by a grunt in the field when not wearing his steel pot.

BUSHMASTER—Jungle warfare expert or soldier skilled in jungle navigation. Also a large deadly snake not common to Vietnam but mighty tasty.

C AND C—Command and Control aircraft that circled overhead to direct the combined air and ground operations.

CAO BOI—Cowboys. A term that referred to the criminals of Saigon who rode motorcycles.

CARIBOU—Cargo transport plane.

CHINOOK—Army Aviation twin-engine helicopter. A CH-47. Also known as a shit hook.

CHOCK—Refers to the number of the aircraft in the flight. Chock Three is the third. Chock Six is the sixth.

CLAYMORE—Antipersonnel mine that fires seven hundred and fifty steel balls with a lethal range of fifty meters.

CLOSE AIR SUPPORT—Use of airplanes and helicopters to fire on enemy units near friendlies.

CO CONG—Female Vietcong.

COLT—Soviet-built small transport plane. The NATO code name for Soviet and Warsaw Pact transports all begin with the letter *C*.

CONEX—Steel container about ten feet high, ten feet wide and ten feet long used to haul equipment and supplies.

DAC CONG—Enemy sappers who attacked in the front ranks to blow up the wire so that the infantry could assault a camp.

DAI UY—Vietnamese army rank equivalent to captain.

DEROS—Date Estimated Return from Overseas Service.

DIRNSA—Director, National Security Agency.

E AND E—Escape and Evasion.

FEET WET—Term used by pilots to describe flight over water.

FIRECRACKER—Special artillery shell that explodes into a number of small bomblets that detonate later. It is the artillery version of the cluster bomb and was a secret weapon employed tactically for the first time at Khe Sanh.

FIVE—Radio call sign for the executive officer of a unit.

FNG—Fucking New Guy.

FOB—Forward Operating Base.

FOX MIKE—FM radio.

FREEDOM BIRD—Name given to any aircraft that took troops out of Vietnam. Usually referred to the commercial jet flights that took men back to the World.

GARAND—M-1 rifle that was replaced by the M-14. Issued to the Vietnamese early in the war.

GO-TO-HELL RAG—Towel or any large cloth worn around the neck by a grunt.

GRAIL—NATO name for shoulder-fired SA-7 surface-to-air missile.

GUARD THE RADIO—Term that means standing by in the commo bunker and listening for messages.

GUIDELINE—NATO name for SA-2 surface-to-air missile.

GUNSHIP—Armed helicopter or cargo plane that carries weapons instead of cargo.

HE—High-explosive ammunition.

HOOTCH—Almost any shelter, from temporary to long-term.

HORN—Term referring to a specific kind of radio operations that used satellites to rebroadcast messages.

HORSE—See *Biscuit*.

HOTEL THREE—Helicopter landing area at Saigon's Tan Son Nhut Airport.

HUEY—UH-1 helicopter.

ICS—Official name for the intercom system in an aircraft.

IN-COUNTRY—Term used to refer to American troops operating in South Vietnam. They were all in-country.

INTELLIGENCE—Any information about enemy operations. It can include troop movements, weapons capabilities, biographies of enemy commanders and general information about terrain features. It is any information that would be useful in planning a mission.

KA-BAR—Type of military combat knife.

KIA—Killed In Action. (Since the U.S. wasn't engaged in a declared war, the use of the term KIA wasn't authorized. KIA came to mean enemy dead. Americans were KHA, or Killed in Hostile Action.)

KLICK—One thousand meters. A kilometer.

LIMA LIMA—Land Line. Refers to telephone communications between two points on the ground.

LLDB—Luc Luong Dac Biet. The South Vietnamese Special Forces. Sometimes referred to as the Look Long, Duck Back.

LSA—Lubricant used by soldiers on their weapons to ensure that they continue to operate properly.

LP—Listening Post. A position outside the perimeter manned by a couple of people to give advance warning of enemy activity.

LRRP—Long Range Reconnaissance Patrol. A special patrol of highly skilled jungle fighters who went in search of the enemy.

LZ—Landing Zone.

M-3A1—Also known as a grease gun. A .45-caliber submachine gun favored in World War II by GIs. Its slow rate of fire meant the barrel didn't rise. As well, the user didn't burn through his ammo as fast as he did in some of his other weapons.

M-14—Standard rifle of the U.S. Army, eventually replaced by the M-16. It fires the standard NATO round—7.62 mm.

M-16—Became the standard infantry weapon of the Vietnam War. It fires 5.56 mm ammunition.

M-79—Short-barreled, shoulder-fired weapon that fires a 40 mm grenade. These can be high explosives, white phosphorus or canister.

M-113—Numerical designation of an armored personnel carrier.

MACV—Military Assistance Command, Vietnam, replaced MAAG in 1964.

MAD MINUTE—Specified time at a base camp when the men in the bunkers would clear their weapons. It came to mean the random firing of all the camp's weapons just as fast as everyone could shoot.

MATCU—Marine Air Traffic Control Unit.

MEDEVAC—Also called Dust-off. A helicopter used to take wounded to medical facilities.

MI—Military Intelligence.

MIA—Missing In Action.

MONOPOLY MONEY—Term used by servicemen in Vietnam to describe the MPC handed out in lieu of regular U.S. currency.

MOS—Military Occupation Specialty. A job description.

MPC—Military Payment Certificates. Used by military in lieu of U.S. dollars.

NCO—A noncommissioned officer. A noncom. A sergeant.

NCOIC—NCO In Charge. The senior NCO in a unit, detachment or patrol.

NDB—Nondirectional beacon. A radio beacon that can be used for homing.

NEXT—The man who said it was his turn next to be rotated home. See *Short*.

NINETEEN—Average age of combat soldier in Vietnam, as opposed to twenty-six in World War II.

NOUC MAM—Foul-smelling sauce used by Vietnamese.

NVA—North Vietnamese Army. Also used to designate a soldier from North Vietnam.

ONTOS—Marine weapon that consists of six 106 mm recoilless rifles mounted on a tracked vehicle.

P(PIASTER)—Basic monetary unit in South Vietnam, worth slightly less than a penny.

PETA-PRIME—Tarlike substance that melted in the heat of the day to become a sticky black nightmare that clung to boots, clothes and equipment. It was used to hold down dust during the dry season.

PETER PILOT—Copilot in a helicopter.

PLF—Parachute Landing Fall. The roll used by parachutists on landing.

POW—Prisoner Of War.

PRC-10—Portable radio.

PRC-25—Lighter portable radio that replaced the PRC-10.

PULL PITCH—Term used by helicopter pilots that means they are going to take off.

PUNJI STAKE—Sharpened bamboo hidden to penetrate the foot. Sometimes dipped in feces.

PUZZLE PALACE—Term referring to the Pentagon. It was called the puzzle palace because no one knew what was going on in it. The Puzzle Palace East referred to MACV or USARV Headquarters in Saigon.

REDLEGS—Term that refers to artillerymen. It derives from the old Army where artillerymen wore red stripes on the legs of their uniforms.

REMF—Rear-Echelon Motherfucker.

RINGKNOCKER—Graduate of a military academy. The term refers to the ring worn by all graduates.

RON—Remain Overnight. Term used by flight crews to indicate a flight that would last longer than a day.

RPD—Soviet-made 7.62 mm light machine gun.

RTO—Radio Telephone Operator. The radio man of a unit.

RUFF-PUFFS—Term applied to the RF-PFs, the regional and popular forces. Militia drawn from the local population.

S-3—Company level operations officer. He is the same as the G-3 on a general's staff.

SA-2—Surface-to-air missile fired from a fixed site. It is a radar-guided missile nearly thirty-five feet long.

SA-7—Surface-to-air missile that is shoulder-fired and has infrared homing.

SACSA—Special Assistant for Counterinsurgency and Special Activities.

SAFE AREA—Selected Area For Evasion. It doesn't mean that the area is safe from the enemy, only that the terrain, location or local population make the area a good place for escape and evasion.

SAM TWO—Refers to the SA-2 Guideline.

SAR—Search and Rescue. SAR forces were the people involved in search-and-rescue missions.

SEALS—The Navy's Special Forces. The name comes from where they fight. On the *S*ea, in the *A*ir and on the *L*and.

SECDEF—Secretary of Defense.

SHORT—Term used by a soldier in Vietnam to tell all who would listen that his turn was almost over.

SHORT-TIME—GI term for a quickie.

SHORT-TIMER—Person who had been in Vietnam for nearly a year and who would be rotated back to the World soon. When the DEROS (Date of Estimated Return from Overseas Service) was the shortest in the unit, the person was said to be next.

SINGLE-DIGIT MIDGET—Soldier with fewer than ten days left in-country.

SIX—Radio call sign for the unit commander.

SKS—Soviet-made carbine.

SMG—Submachine gun.

SOI—Signal Operating Instructions. The booklet that contained the call signs and radio frequencies of the units in Vietnam.

SOP—Standard Operating Procedure.

SPIKE TEAM—Special Forces team made up for a direct-action mission.

STEEL POT—Standard U.S. Army helmet. The steel pot was the outer metal cover.

TAOR—Tactical Area of Operational Responsibility.

TEAM UNIFORM OR COMPANY UNIFORM—UHF radio frequency on which the team or the company communicates. Frequencies were changed periodically in an attempt to confuse the enemy.

THE WORLD—The United States.

THREE—Radio call sign of the operations officer.

THREE CORPS—Military area around Saigon. Vietnam was divided into four corps areas.

TO&E—Table of Organization and Equipment. A detailed listing of all the men and equipment assigned to a unit.

TOC—Tactical Operations Center.

TOT—Time Over Target. Refers to the time an aircraft is supposed to be over the drop zone with the parachutists, or the target if the plane is a bomber.

TRICK CHIEF—NCOIC for a shift.

TRIPLE A—Antiaircraft Artillery or AAA. This is anything used to shoot at airplanes and helicopters.

TWO—Radio call sign of the intelligence officer.

TWO-OH-ONE (201) FILE—Military records file that listed all of a soldier's qualifications, training, experience and abilities. It was passed from unit to unit so that the new commander would have some idea about the capabilities of an incoming soldier.

UMZ—Ultramilitarized Zone. Name GIs gave to the DMZ (Demilitarized Zone).

UNIFORM—Refers to the UHF radio. Company Uniform would be the frequency assigned to that company.

USARV—United States Army, Vietnam.

VC—Vietcong, called Victor Charlie (phonetic alphabet) or just Charlie.

VIETCONG—Contraction of Vietnam Cong San (Vietnamese Communist).

VIETCONG SAN—Vietnamese Communist. A term in use since 1956.

WHITE MICE—Referred to the South Vietnamese military police because they all wore white helmets.

WIA—Wounded In Action.

WILLIE PETE—WP, white phosphorus, called smoke rounds. Also used as antipersonnel weapons.

WSO—Weapons System Officer. The name given to the man who rode in the back seat of a Phantom because he was responsible for the weapons systems.

XO—Executive officer of a unit.

ZAP—To ding, pop caps or shoot. To kill.

From Europe to Africa, the Executioner stalks his elusive enemy—a cartel of ruthless men who might prove too powerful to defeat.

DON PENDLETON's
MACK BOLAN

Moving Target

One of America's most powerful corporations is reaping huge profits by dealing in arms with anyone who can pay the price. Dogged by assassins, Mack Bolan follows his only lead fast and hard—and becomes caught up in a power struggle that might be his last.

Phoenix Force—bonded in secrecy to avenge the acts of terrorists everywhere.

Super Phoenix Force #2

American ''killer'' mercenaries are involved in a KGB plot to overthrow the government of a South Pacific island. The American President, anxious to preserve his country's image and not disturb the precarious position of the island nation's government, sends in the experts—Phoenix Force—to prevent a coup.